Caramel Kisses

CHILDLESS, MICHAEL GRAY longs to find the daughter his deceased wife gave up for adoption years ago. His search takes a detour when he meets candy maker Dara Greene. Dara is also widowed and she's determined to make her business, Caroline's Candy Shoppe, a success. But Dara suffers from stage fright and due to a recent traumatic event, she seeks Michael's assistance. Can he help her win the Annual Cruise Ship Candy Competition and convince her to take a chance on love?

CARAMEL KISSES
The Candy Beach Series
Copyright © 2018 by Cecelia Dowdy

Interior Format

Caramel KISSES

THE CANDY BEACH SERIES

Cecelia Dowdy

PRAISE FOR
CECELIA DOWDY'S WRITING

Dowdy writes with the right touch to keep the readers engaged and vested…
  ~ USA Today

CHAPTER 1

MIMI DIDN'T DESERVE this, heck, nobody did, but especially not Mimi…not *his* Mimi. Michael Gray fingered the crisp white sheet before sliding his hand underneath and grasping her wrinkled fingers. He gripped the railing of the hospice bed with his other hand. He sniffed. The vivid scents of rubbing alcohol and antiseptic filled the air as he studied her small chest barely moving. She breathed from the oxygen tubes through her nose. He briefly glanced at their wedding picture which was displayed beside her bed. They'd been in love, young and he'd just joined the Navy.

He focused on Mimi again. Her vitals were no longer stable and hospice had called him, letting him know that she didn't have much time left. That's why he'd rushed over as soon as he could. He eased into the chair beside the bed and continued holding her hand. Her eyes fluttered open. Her dark brown eyes focused on him with unusual clarity. "Michael." Just hearing his name softly uttered from her sweet lips made his heart skip.

"Don't talk, Mimi." She barely nodded and closed her eyes. Her nut-brown skin looked a bit waxy and laugh lines fanned from her eyes. Up until a few months ago, his Mimi was always laughing, happy, talkative. She loved running the bakery with him, and she made a mean batch of candy. They'd often sold her candies, right beside their baked goods, in their privately-owned bakery. Although they'd been married forty years, she still shooed him from the kitchen whenever she made her candy. She still kept her recipe a secret from him after all these years. At sixty-eight, his Mimi would be breathing her last breath, passing on into heaven, within the next few hours, according to hospice.

"Michael?" she struggled to open her eyes again. The staff had warned him over the last few weeks that his Mimi would not be herself due to the level of medications that they were giving her.

"Honey, don't talk." Thankfully, her eyes closed again. He studied her, the memories rushing through his mind like warm sunshine. He recalled the first time he met Emilia Rose Sanderson. It was back in 1963 during the March for Civil Rights in Washington. They'd only been sixteen years old and he'd been enamored with her smooth brown skin and deep, soulful eyes. With her sultry voice, full of courage, she'd told him she was called Mimi. As they'd fought for civil rights, he'd thought of her as *his* Mimi. They'd married two years later and had been together ever since.

So many years…so many memories. They'd shared so much. He continued clutching her hand. Salty wetness slid down his cheeks. So many good years. He stood on his shaky legs and kissed her cheek. Yes, he'd spent most of his life with his Mimi. It had been a good marriage. His only regret was that they'd never been blessed with any children. He squeezed his eyes shut, unable to stop the stream of tears. He'd imagine his grief wouldn't be as raw if he'd had children and grandchildren who'd loved Mimi, too.

"Michael." She mumbled his name again. "Listen…to…me." He lowered his ear toward her lips. "Baby…I have baby."

A baby. What in the world was she talking about? They'd never had any children so maybe she was confused. She was probably thinking of all the time and effort they'd put into trying to have a child. "Mimi, it's okay. You're confused. Just close your eyes and get some rest."

"No." She grabbed his hand with surprising strength. "Baby. Make sure baby is okay. Bank. Safe deposit at the bank." She then dropped his hand and closed her eyes.

She had a baby? How could that be? As his Mimi stopped breathing, tears slid down his cheeks. *Lord, I'm so hurt and confused right now. Please help me with this pain. Amen.*

CHAPTER 2

Three years later…

"THAT'S EXACTLY WHAT we need, Susan. A candy-making machine." Seventy-year-old Dara Greene sipped from her large mug of coffee as she gestured toward the screen of her laptop. The video displayed a large round steel machine that gleamed in the sunlight. Beach tourists flocked to the large bay window of the candy shop and ogled at the homemade candy that bubbled in the cauldron like hot thick soup. The mixture was poured into a large tray to cool. Then, once it was cooled, another machine was used to cut the caramels into neat, even pieces. The entire process was like magic and folks seemed to enjoy it. She'd watched this video, and several others like it, over the last week.

She glanced around the tidy office nestled in the back of her candy shop. The sweet, aromatic scent of her homemade vanilla caramels filled the air with sweetness. She put her mug aside, and squeezed her sore brown fingers. Her arthritis had been acting up lately. Well, after she took some medicine, she was sure her fingers would be nimble enough to make more of the candy that they'd need for the customers that day.

Her business partner and accountant, Susan, glanced down at their financial statements before refocusing on the computer screen.

Her friend rubbed her forehead.

"Susan, are you okay? You don't look good." She'd been complaining about not feeling well over the last couple of weeks. Dara had urged her to go to the doctor and Susan had promised she'd go. "Have you made your doctor's appointment yet?"

"No. I've been too busy." She gestured around the office. "We've been busy trying to get our business out of the red."

"Well, we're not too busy to take care of ourselves. Are you sick?"

"I'm not feeling well. I've got a killer headache."

"You should go home. I can handle things by myself today."

Susan's mouth pinched with apparent pain. "Could you bring me a glass of water, please?"

Dara rushed to get Susan's drink. She presented her with a cup of ice water. Susan opened her purse and removed two pills and swallowed them, chasing them with the water. "Thanks. I feel so sick that I don't feel like standing up right now."

She patted her friend's shoulder. "You need to

take better care of yourself. Why don't I give you a lift home and you can lie down and take a nap? Or better yet, why don't I take you to the urgent care center?"

Susan squeezed her eyes shut. "That's okay. My headache should be gone in a few minutes." She opened her eyes and gestured toward the screen, her face still pinched with pain. "Dara, I don't know about this machine. It's a good idea. But I've crunched the numbers and I just don't think we can afford it right now." She had always envied Susan's intelligence. While Dara had gotten married right out of high school, had a passel of kids and never worked, her best friend had gone to college and had gotten her bachelors and master's degrees. Susan had done it all, gotten married, had kids and had had an amazing career as a CPA.

Now, both of them were seventy years old and widowed. They'd been running their own candy shop, Caroline's Candy Shoppe, for three years. When Dara had purchased the shop with her husband's life insurance money, she'd named the shop after Caroline, her grandmother, the happiest and best candy maker she'd ever known.

"Listen, Susan, I know you'd warned that it would probably take five years for us to be profitable but, we don't have that kind of time. Since a competing candy shop has moved down the street, our sales have declined and I don't want to lose any more business."

"Yes, I did say that. But, you can't just make money appear out of nowhere. We're already stretched too thin as it is. Plus, we had to hire a new person to help with our summer rush of customers." She checked her watch. "Where is our new employee anyway?" She winced with pain again.

"Why don't you come upstairs and lie down?" Dara's living quarters were on the second floor of the shop. "You could take a nap and I'll wake you up later."

Susan took a deep breath. "I'll be fine. Where's our new employee?" she asked again.

She sighed. "She didn't show up. I hired her a week ago and told her to report to work early today. That's teenagers for you. Some of them cannot be depended on."

"Well, we'll need to hire someone to help us with our summer rush of customers." She then gestured toward the computer screen again. "Back to what we were discussing. I just can't justify purchasing a thirty-thousand-dollar candy machine when I don't really know if it'll increase our profitability. Just because that machine increased the profitability for that European shop doesn't mean it would work for us."

"Can't we get a loan to finance it?" She was determined to get that machine. Deep in her gut, she felt that it would make a great addition to their business. Their competitor didn't even have a large store-front window facing the beach. Besides, their competitor's candy didn't taste nearly as good as hers. Her candy was sweet, exquisite and tasty. One of their customers had said it tasted like a slice of heaven – what a way to describe candy.

Susan shrugged. "Maybe, maybe not. But thirty thousand dollars is a lot to gamble." She wiped her hand across her sweaty forehead. She took several deep breaths. "I wasn't sure if we stood a chance, but, I wanted to tell you about—" Her face slacked and her eyes glazed.

"Susan!" Her friend dropped from the chair, hitting her head on the floor. Blood oozed from her head wound and she moved her mouth, but, could not speak.

Dara's heart pounded as she dropped to the floor. She cradled Susan's head while she dialed 911.

CHAPTER 3

MICHAEL GRAY'S HEART thudded as he slammed the brake of his car. Abandoned. The grass in front of the ramshackle beach cottage stood at least a foot high. A long crack slashed across the front window. The peeling paint blistered under the early morning sun. The broken screen door flapped in the wind. He squeezed his eyes shut. He finally opened his eyes and stared at the forlorn-looking home. *Lord, Mimi has been gone for three years and I'm still grieving for her. This is the last address that the private detective had on file for Mimi's daughter, Amy Bluestone.*

His wife had given birth to Amy Bluestone when she was fifteen years old. She'd then immediately given her up for adoption. The only reason he knew Amy Bluestone's name was because of the private detective that he'd hired. When Mimi told him about her baby she didn't even know the child's name. He still had a hard time imagining Mimi having a baby. Since they'd never been able to have children of their own he'd mistakenly assumed his wife was simply not able to have kids.

He checked the clock on his dashboard. It was only six AM. He took a deep breath and yawned. He'd been driving all night. His insomnia had gotten worse over the last three years. When he'd told his church folks about his sleeping problem, they'd been shocked. They'd never known a man his age to have trouble sleeping. Well, ever since Mimi died, it was like he could not get used to living without her.

He slowly got out of the car. His knees creaked. He stood up straight and tried to ease the crick in his back. At seventy-one, he considered himself in good shape for his age. But, when he sat for a long time, he felt as if his bones lost all flexibility. He slowly flexed his foot and finally moseyed over to the ramshackle beach cottage. The tall grass swayed in the early morning breeze as sand dusted his sandaled feet. A sharp movement from his right caused the grass to bend. He frowned. Some critter must be hiding out in that grass. He leaned forward and studied the house through the smeared dirty windows.

Nothing. Well, nothing much. Pieces of wood and trash covered the living room floor. Well, he supposed it was the living room. He turned away from the dreadful sight to study the front porch. Broken lawn furniture littered the porch. He ambled over to the back yard and spotted an old tire swing hanging from a huge oak tree. Puzzled, he returned to his car. He removed his sandals and glanced down the quiet neighborhood street.

He then focused on the cottage he'd be renting – right next door to where Amy supposedly lived. When he'd contacted a Realtor about Crystal Beach rentals he'd been stunned that the cottage next door to Mimi's daughter was available for the summer. Apparently, there'd been a last-minute cancellation. So, after he'd gotten a neighbor to watch his house in Twinkle, Maryland he signed a lease to rent the cottage next door to Amy's for the entire summer. Granted, he knew it was weird, downright strange, to be living in a house right next to Amy when he'd not even met her yet.

But, he figured that he couldn't just mosey up to the woman, introduce himself and then tell her about his wife. He couldn't call her since her residence didn't have a phone number. He'd thought and prayed about Mimi's baby over the last three years. After Mimi had died, he'd been haunted by her death. Downright missed her so much that it felt like a razor-sharp knife pierced right into his soul. He'd privately cried buckets of tears…he always cried in private. He never let anybody see him cry, not in his entire life…well, that wasn't true.

The only person he'd ever allowed to see him cry was Mimi. Just being with her completed him. He didn't hide any secrets from his wife.

But, Mimi had hidden a doozy of a secret. After he'd discovered that she had a child, he'd felt hurt and betrayed. Why did she wait until she was on her deathbed to tell him about the baby? Were there other secrets she was hiding, and if so, what? Did he really *know* his wife? He'd discovered she'd not only had a kid, but, she'd had a secret bank account. Money she was saving to give to the child she'd given up for adoption.

He glanced at his watch. Well, the Realtor's wouldn't be open for another few hours, so, he had some time to kill before he went to the real estate office to get the key to his rental. In the meantime, he'd take a nice long walk on the beach, that's what he'd do. As he moved toward the crashing waves, memories of Mimi's death clouded his mind. He wiggled his dark, wrinkled toes in the sand. He took a deep breath as he continued walking along the shore. He raised his head toward the rising sun and enjoyed the exquisite warmth. Seagulls flew in the early morning sky and young birds frolicked near the water, fighting over a piece of bread that someone had tossed.

He relished the echo of the waves crashing onto the shore. Oh, how he loved the crisp clean scent of the salty water. It was almost as if God were trying to sooth his troubled mood with the ocean. He sighed and continued walking.

He stopped and sniffed. The scent of cigarette smoke tickled his nose. He turned around. A beach bum wandered close behind. Shirtless, his massive stomach hung over his swim trunks while he chugged from a bottle of whiskey. He slid the cigarette between his thick lips and took a long drag. Who'd get wasted so early in the morning? Well, he had no room to judge.

The bum peered directly into his eyes and offered the bottle. "Want some?" His mouth watered. Yes, he'd love some, but, he knew better. He'd given up drinking and smoking when he'd become saved. The man shoved the bottle toward him. "You want some. I can tell by the way you're looking at it."

Right after Mimi died he'd broken his sobriety for an entire month. He'd hit rock bottom. Visions of his puking over an open toilet and smoking a pack of cigarettes a day...he'd hoped the alcohol and nicotine would dull the pain. But, when he sobered up the pain was still raw and fresh. He'd found it had taken time and a lot of support from his church family to see him through the darkest days of his life.

The strong scent of the alcohol wafted toward him and beckoned him to take a sip. He shook his head. "No. You need something to eat or drink?" He figured this bum may need a hot meal and a drink of water. Smelled like he needed a bath, too.

The middle-aged man shook his head before he ambled away. Michael frowned. Just seeing that bum brought back painful memories. No, he'd never been homeless, but he'd come close to losing his bakery while he dealt with his pain. He'd finally sold the bakery a couple of years after Mimi's death. He'd befriended Kelly and Jamal, a young married couple, and he felt like his business had been left in good hands.

Since he was retired and sober he needed to fulfill Mimi's wishes. He'd re-hired the same private investigator that Mimi had initially used to find Amy. He told the PI to resume his search and he was so glad that he did. Now that he was in Crystal Beach his search for Amy should soon be completed.

He sniffed. His mind had to be playing tricks. His mind had been so consumed about Mimi and the baby…well, baby was probably the wrong word. Mimi's baby would be about fifty-five right now. He needed to stop thinking about this woman as an infant.

He sniffed again. Yep, he really must be imagining things. The scent of chocolate, brown sugar and vanilla tickled the warm humid air with exquisite sweetness. He blinked away the sheen of tears in his old eyes as he took another whiff. His Mimi…just the smell of that sweetness made him recall his deceased wife. Smelled like a batch of her candy was baking.

He followed the delicious scent with his nose. He finally spotted the source of the amazing smell on this early Saturday morning. Caroline's Candy Shoppe. Blue, bright and colorful, the large front window of the shop shined in the early morning light. He followed the short path to the candy shop.

Whew, what a walk. He felt the sweat clinging to his face as he trekked to the bench right outside the shop. He gulped several deep breaths, winded. Whew, he wasn't getting any younger. He needed to stop and rest for a bit. Walking on that beach made him tired.

He dropped onto the bench to rest for a spell.

The scent of the wonderful candy surrounded him. The piercing wail of a siren interrupted his thoughts. He studied the ambulance pulling up to the candy shop. He spotted a distraught, elderly, petite brown woman who rushed to the two EMTs and beckoned them into the candy shop. "Mimi." He muttered the name as if he were actually seeing his deceased wife.

But, that wasn't Mimi. This had happened to him a few times over the last three years. He'd see a familiar-looking woman and for a split second, he'd think it was Mimi. It only took him a moment to recall that Mimi was dead. The few moments of seeing a person who looked like Mimi…well…it was like fresh water to his battered soul. *Lord, help me with my pain.*

The Mimi-lookalike sobbed while the paramedics carried out a person on a stretcher. His heart lurched – just seeing the ambulance and seeing the paramedics brought back memories of when his Mimi had first collapsed, right before they'd discovered she'd had cancer. "Ah, Mimi."

The Mimi-lookalike seemed to have heard him. She turned and looked directly at him. Her sad dark eyes pierced directly into his soul. His mouth dropped open. Had she heard him say the name Mimi? Was Mimi *her* name too? He blinked a few times before he heard the screech of the siren as the ambulance pulled away. The quick glance he'd shared with the woman couldn't have been more than a second.

He sighed. Memories of Mimi continued to surround him. *Lord, when will the pain from Mimi's death go away? Please help me to find her daughter so that I can move on with my life. Amen.*

CHAPTER 4

STILL RATTLED ABOUT seeing someone who looked like Mimi, he slowly started the journey back to Amy's house. While he walked he took note of the friendly atmosphere of Crystal Beach. A thriving boardwalk boasted several restaurants, bars, and hotels. Several families exited the hotels sporting sunglasses and beachwear. He noticed several beachcombers lazing near the water while they applied sunscreen. Several folks waved. He stopped and took in his surroundings. Crystal Beach seemed like a nice, friendly place. Good thing he'd made the decision to stay for the summer. He could really get used to living in a place like this.

As he approached Amy's house, he zeroed in on the tall, lanky light-skinned young Black man mowing the lawn in front of Amy's abandoned cottage. He also spotted cans of white paint sitting on the curb and boxes of flowers that he assumed were going to be planted in the broken flowerboxes. Well, since he needed to find Amy, this was probably the best way to start.

He stopped at his car and got his sandals. He then slid the shoes onto his bare feet. As he waved to the young man, he smelled the delicious, hickory scent of bacon and the subtle scent of toasted bread. Smelled like folks in this neighborhood were early risers who liked to cook breakfast in the morning. He fondly recalled how he'd wake up early on Sunday mornings and he and Mimi would share a long, lazy breakfast before church.

The man mowing the lawn wiped his sweaty brow as he turned and focused on Michael. "Hey!" Michael called out, waving to the young man again.

He figured the man couldn't hear him over the loud roar of the mower. He cut off the motor before focusing on Michael again. "Hi, can I help you?"

Michael nodded and approached him. He breathed in the aroma of freshly mowed grass as he offered his hand. "I'm Michael Gray. I rented the cottage next door. I'll be living here for the summer."

The young man wiped his hands on his pants before shaking Michael's hand. "Pleased to meet you. I'm Lyle Greene." The young man's face was covered with freckles. He stood up straighter. "Looks like we're neighbors. I live next door, too." Well, imagine that. Looked like he lived on one side of Amy's home and Michael lived on the other side. "So, you're staying here for the entire summer?"

Michael nodded. "I apologize for interrupting. But, I have a problem and I'm hoping you can help me."

"I can try. What's up?"

"Well, I'm looking for a woman named Amy Bluestone. She used to live right here." He gestured toward the abandoned cottage. "She's in her mid-fifties, Black woman. I figured since you were mowing her lawn, you might know her."

Lyle slowly shook his head. His kinky light brown hair gleamed under the bright sunshine. "I recently moved into the house next door. Since I've been here, this house," he pointed towards Amy's home, "has been empty."

Well, that's not what he wanted to hear. This man looked to be about his mid-twenties. He seemed friendly enough, so, Michael felt comfortable asking him some more probing questions. Heck, he'd do whatever he could to find Mimi's daughter. "Well, why are you mowing the lawn? I'd assume whomever lived here would've hired you."

Lyle grinned. "Looks like you're mighty anxious to find Amy."

Well, he might as well tell this young man the truth. As of right now, he seemed to be the best option for finding Amy. Besides, at seventy-one, he'd discovered that he'd developed a good judge of character over the years. He sensed that Lyle was open and friendly. The man gave him a good feeling and he figured Lyle would help him if he could. "My wife died three years ago."

Lyle frowned. His brown eyes were kind as he

speared him with a direct look. "I'm sorry." He clapped him on the shoulder. "Is that why you came to the beach for the summer? You needed to get away to get over your wife's death?"

He quickly explained why he needed to find Amy. "So, I wonder why you're mowing the lawn since this is where Amy used to live and…" he again gestured toward the sad-looking house. "It appears that nobody lives here. I just need help finding her and I figure you might know somebody who can help me."

"The owner of the house hired me to mow the lawn and to paint the house. I believe he's planning to rent it out. He's out of the country, been living abroad for over six months." He folded his arms in front of his chest. "He's mad at the folks who used to live here. I'm assuming Amy is one of the people he's angry with."

Michael frowned. "What do you mean?"

"Well, apparently, they broke their lease and moved out. They owed him three months' rent and left the place a mess." He gestured for Michael to follow him. They plopped down on the steps and Lyle opened a small cooler. A few bottles of water nested in the tub of ice. He offered one to Michael before popping off the top and guzzling it down in a few minutes. Looked like he was mighty thirsty.

As Michael drank his water, Lyle opened a second bottle of water and guzzled it just as quickly. He then wiped his mouth with the back of his hand. "I work at the hardware store downtown. I'm also starting my own business as a handyman.

I can fix most anything and I also mow lawns. The owner of this house found out that I was starting my own business and he contacted me to fix up the cottage. He's paying me top dollar to have the outside of this place fixed up. It was like God was smiling down on me when I landed this job because I need the money."

Michael raised his eyebrows when Lyle mentioned God. "Yes, I know what you mean."

Lyle grinned. "Yes, the Lord works mysteriously. That's for sure." He paused and glanced at his water bottle, apparently in deep thought. His phone buzzed. "Hi, Grandma." He gripped the phone. "I'll be right there." He shoved his phone into his pocket. "I have to go." The urgency of his words put an end to their conversation. Lyle rushed to the tan SUV parked in front of his house. Michael stood. What could've happened to rattle him so much? The motor of Lyle's car sputtered. Michael ambled over to the car and eyed Lyle attempting to start the vehicle. Michael rapped against the closed window and caught Lyle's attention. The young man opened the door.

"If you need a lift someplace, I'm happy to take you."

Lyle quickly nodded as he got out of the car and slammed the door. "Yeah, could you take me to Crystal Beach Memorial Hospital? I just found out a good friend of mine had a stroke and I need to go see her."

As he ushered Lyle over to his car, he recalled the ambulance he'd spotted moments ago. He wondered if the victim was someone who worked in the candy shop.

Dara paced as fast as her old tired legs could go. She wrung her hands. A stroke. Susan, her best friend, had gone and had a stroke. She wasn't allowed to go back and see her yet. Upset, she'd called her grandson Lyle. She knew she could count on him to get the word out to all their church friends about Susan. Lyle often helped out at the candy shop when they were short-staffed.

Lyle rushed through the doors of the waiting room. He hugged her tight. "How's Aunt Susan?" Susan wasn't really his aunt, but, since she was her best friend, and Lyle had known her his entire life, he just called her Aunt Susan. Tears streamed from his eyes. He swiped the moisture away with his hand. His light brown skin reddened. Her grandson's skin always got red when he was nervous or upset.

"Oh, Lyle. I don't know. They won't tell me anything." She happened to glance over and spot the man she'd seen earlier. She swallowed, suddenly realizing he stared at her.

Lyle gently led her over to the good-looking stranger. He'd said the name Mimi when he'd spotted her earlier. Weird that she'd remember that when she'd been so distressed while getting into the ambulance with Susan. "This is Michael Gray. He's renting the house two doors down from me. My car wouldn't start. He offered me a ride over. Michael, this is my grandmother, Dara Greene."

His dark eyes seemed to pierce deep into her soul as they shook hands. "Sorry to have to meet you under such circumstances, ma'am."

Ma'am? Why'd he call her that? This man had to be at least as old as she was. She shook the thought away. "Please, call me Dara. Thanks for giving Lyle a ride over."

He nodded. "Much obliged to do so."

A man wearing scrubs breezed through the doors and came toward them. She breathed with relief. Finally, an update. "So, how is Susan doing?"

"Ma'am, I can't reveal information to you unless you're family."

Dara huffed and stood taller. "Well, I'm her best friend. She's like a sister to me."

The doctor shook his head. "I can't release information about the patient to non-family members."

Lyle, bless his heart, put his arms around her. Sometimes, she didn't know what she'd do without her strong, loving grandson around. "Grandma, have you called any of her kids or grandkids?"

She'd been so anxious since this happened that she'd not been thinking clearly. She needed to stop thinking of her emotional pain and think of Susan's family. Her children and grandchildren didn't know that their relative had had a stroke. Her hands shook as she pulled her phone from her pocket. She handed it to Lyle. "Could you call them for me? I'm such an emotional wreck right now."

Lyle led her over to a chair and she plopped down into it. Her head hurt and her joints ached with pain. She needed a dose of Aleve. Lyle's strong voice sounded soothing and comforting while he calmly called Susan's relatives.

She rubbed her forehead and glanced up. Apparently, Michael had left the waiting room and was now returning. He balanced a small cardboard tray with three coffees. He also had muffins, too. His thoughtful generosity made her smile. He placed the tray on the table and stood. "Bought you a little something, just in case. I figure you all might be here for a while."

"Thank you." She rubbed her forehead.

"You okay? Need some aspirin or something?"

"My Aleve. It helps with my sore joints and my headaches. I left it back home."

She eyed Michael while he left. He returned minutes later with a small bottle of the medicine. "Got this for you at the pharmacy. Do you need anything else?"

She accepted the pills. "No, thank you. I appreciate this." She took the medicine as Michael patiently stood nearby. It was strange having him there as if he belonged. She wondered when Lyle had met this kind man. Lyle continued to talk on the phone. He finally returned her phone back to her.

"I just finished talking to Ms. Susan's granddaughter. She'll be here in a few minutes so that we can get an update on Susan's condition. She said she'd let the rest of the family know. Some of them are out of town, so, it may be awhile before everybody gets here." He paused and stared at the floor. "She was crying when I was talking to her. Her husband had to calm her down. He said he'd be driving her over."

Michael lifted a pad of paper and a pen from the table. He wrote something down before handing the paper to Lyle. "Since you don't have transportation, you can call me if you need me to come pick you up. I reckon it's best I leave. Not sure if it's right for me to stay during a family matter."

Dara's headache slowly evaporated and the ache in her joints melted away. As the medicine she'd recently taken started to work, she eyed Michael as he strolled out of the hospital. She closed her eyes and about a half hour later, Lyle shook her awake. She looked up and spotted Susan's grand-daughter rushing into the waiting room, her husband right beside her. Good, since Susan's family was now here, maybe the doctor would give them a report about her condition.

CHAPTER 5

WHAT A WEEK. He'd only been in Crystal Beach for seven days and so far, he was no closer to finding Amy Bluestone. He'd dropped off Lyle and Dara at the hospital one week ago. Afterwards he'd gotten the key from the realtor for his cottage rental. He'd asked the realtor if he knew Amy Bluestone. The realtor had never heard of Amy, so, he couldn't offer Michael any nuggets of wisdom as to how to find Mimi's daughter.

After he'd unpacked and had gotten settled into his summer cottage, he'd returned to Caroline's Candy Shoppe the following day. Lyle had been working there, helping his grandmother. He'd explained that Dara had been spending most of her days at the hospital with Susan. When Michael had told him about the candy he'd smelled on the day that Susan collapsed, Lyle had patiently explained that he did not make the treats. Dara had been coming in each morning and making the candy before she went to the hospital. He'd merely been working the register and waiting on customers. He did tell Michael that Dara was trying to perfect her recipe for vanilla caramels each morning, so, that was probably what Michael had smelled during the morning of Susan's collapse.

Even though he'd not spoken to Dara since his hospital encounter, he'd seen her around. Lyle had invited him to his church that week. As a result, he'd been going to Crystal Beach Community Church each night. They were having a revival all week, and every night they had a guest preacher. He'd spotted Dara sitting in the back. He'd watched out for her. She'd always slip in after church started and sit in the back pew. She'd then quietly slip out right before the end of the service.

He'd toyed with the idea of sitting back there with her. The last pew was usually empty and he kind of wanted to sit beside her. But, he sensed she'd wanted to be alone. Once he'd glanced back there and caught her wiping away tears. She'd noticed his blatant stare and had looked away. It still shocked him about how much she resembled Mimi from a distance.

Lyle had mentioned that his grandma had been sad since Susan was in the hospital. Hopefully her friend would heal from her stroke. Lyle had also told him that Susan was awake, but, she was not able to speak.

Michael continued to think about Dara, Susan and Lyle as he locked the door to his rental house and strolled down the sidewalk. Lyle had invited

him over for dinner that evening. He was going
to grill some steaks and then they'd be watching the ballgame afterwards. Seemed kind of
strange for a man his age to be hanging out with
a twenty-something man. You'd think they'd have
nothing in common.

But, he found that Lyle was close to his grandmother and he found himself asking questions
about the older woman. Just as he turned the corner and saw Lyle's house in plain view, he spotted
Dara. She was getting out of her car and tears
streamed down her nut-brown face. She clutched
a white box as she tried to wipe her wet eyes.

Dara wiped her eyes. Goodness, this had been
a rough week. She'd spent the better part of the
last week in ICU with Susan. She'd gotten no
sleep the previous night, she'd been up praying
and thinking about her best friend. She'd wanted
to spend the night in the hospital with Susan in
the ICU unit but the staff had said that only one
visitor was allowed overnight with patients.

Susan's distraught granddaughter had spent the
night in the hospital, so, Dara had gone home.
Moving around helped her to ease her worry…
at least it helped some. She'd spent the night
baking a big batch of the caramel candy recipe
she'd been experimenting with. Lyle had noticed
her fatigue and had suggested they share dinner

together that evening. Her grandson could grill a delicious steak. They could enjoy the candy she'd brought for dessert.

"Hello Dara." The deep male voice was right behind her. Startled, she swiftly turned and slammed right into a solid chest. She sniffed and realized her nose was running and tears were streaming down her face. Strong arms came around her, as if protecting her from a fall. Brown male arms held her and didn't let go until she'd regained her balance. She blinked as a cloth square was pressed into her hand.

A handkerchief. It had been years since she'd seen one of those. She was certainly an emotional wreck. She wiped her wet eyes and looked into the elderly face of Michael Gray. Well, this was a surprise indeed. Lyle had not mentioned inviting Michael to dinner. He'd made it appear as if the two of them would be dining alone…hadn't he? She'd been so confused and unfocused lately, worrying about Susan. She may have misunderstood Lyle's invite.

The man cleared his throat. "You look a mite confused right now. Are you okay?"

No, she was bloody awful. But, she was assuming Michael knew this. After all, the last few times he'd seen her, she'd been crying, worrying about her best friend. He probably thought she was a basket case. Well, she was going through a rough time right now, so, she was entitled to some tears. "Just worrying about Susan is all."

"I figured. Saw you over at the church for a few nights, but, sensed you wanted to be alone."

She nodded. Michael was right about that. She wanted to be in church, but, didn't much want to talk to anybody. "How is Susan doing?"

"She's awake but hasn't been able to talk. The hospital says that she may regain her speech through therapy. One side of her body is paralyzed, too."

"I'm sorry."

"Thanks. Please pray for her, and for me too." She needed all the prayers she could get.

"I've been praying for all of you. I'd be much obliged to continue doing that." He gestured toward Lyle's house. "Lyle invited me over to dinner tonight. Looks like he invited you, too."

She nodded. She wanted to mention that she wanted to spend some time alone with her grandson that evening, but, she didn't want to be rude. Michael seemed nice and considerate. He'd probably bow out of having dinner if he knew that she didn't want extra company that evening.

He gently removed the candy box from her hand and their fingers touched. Her skin warmed from the brief contact. He held her box of treats and gently placed his hand in the small of her back, as if giving her emotional and physical support as they made their way to Lyle's screened-in front porch. He opened the screen door and she stepped onto the porch. Michael gently eased the door closed behind them before approaching the front door.

He knocked.

Nobody came to the door. "Lyle it's us." She figured her grandson may have forgotten about their dinner invite, which would be downright strange. Her grandson never forgot anything.

Silence.

Her phone buzzed. She glanced at the display. Lyle. She accepted the call. "Lyle, where are you? Michael and I are here for dinner."

"Sorry grandma. My car broke down."

She signed. "Again? Honey, you really need to look into getting a new car."

"I can't afford one right now. Not until I get my handyman business off the ground. I got my car towed to the garage and a friend of mine is on his way to give me a lift home. You and Michael just sit tight until I get there."

She ended the call and told Michael what Lyle had said. Michael gestured toward the lawn chairs on the porch. "Have a seat." He waited until she'd sat before he eased into the chair beside her. She glanced over at him, caught him staring at her.

Her skin heated and she smiled. She felt like she was sixteen again and out on her first date, which was ludicrous since this wasn't a date at all. She needed to focus on something, anything. She stared at the house across the street. Flowers bloomed from the garden and a wonderful breeze wafted toward them. The air was tinted with the scent of the ocean. The urge to walk on the beach suddenly filled her to the core.

She stole another glance at Michael. He was staring at her box of candy. Well, they might as well take a walk and kill some time until Lyle showed up. "Why don't we take a walk on the beach?" The invite popped out of her mouth before she could stop it.

He raised his eyebrows. "Mind if we munch on your candy while we walk?"

She nodded. "Sure."

A few minutes later they slowly strolled on the beach. The wind whipped around them and seagulls glided in the clear blue sky. Surfers tossed on the ocean waves.

He studied her, still feeling a bit off kilter being around somebody who reminded him so much of his Mimi. She glanced at him and caught him staring at her. His heart pounded with embarrassment. "Sorry for staring."

She shook her head and looked at him quickly. "I vaguely recall seeing you stare at me when the ambulance came for Susan last week."

Well, might as well tell her the truth. No use hiding it. "You favor my wife. She died going on three years now."

"I'm sorry."

He barely managed to nod as he pulled out his phone. He stopped walking as he opened the picture app. He didn't want Dara to think he was some weirdo, making up stories about her resemblance to Mimi. He found Mimi's picture and offered his phone to Dara. "This is Mimi."

Dara accepted the phone and looked down at the picture. Her cute eyebrows raised when she saw the pic. "That really does look like me." Surprise tinged her lovely voice. Feeling a bit nervous, he toyed with the wrapped candy he'd stuffed into his pocket.

Michael focused on Dara again. For the first time in a long while, he felt good...nice. He wasn't sure if it was just the feeling of being near somebody who resembled Mimi, or, if it was because he was on the beach. She returned his phone to him as they continued walking. "I lost my husband, too. A few years ago."

"I'm sorry."

She waved his sympathies away, as if she didn't want to be bothered hearing condolences. Well, he could certainly understand that since he didn't like it when people said they were sorry about Mimi. "I never worked when I was married. When my husband died, I took his life insurance money and opened a candy store."

Michael pulled a piece of candy from his pocket and grinned. "That's why I initially visited your candy store. I smelled your candy. It reminded me of the candy Mimi used to make. We owned a bakery and...well...she was more of a candy maker than a baker. She used to sell her caramels in our bakery. She never did tell me her secret recipe." Unable to resist, he unwrapped the caramel and popped it into his mouth. Delicious buttery sweetness exploded on his tongue like warm sugar. He smacked his lips.

Dara opened her mouth and laughed. Her loud laughter carried over the warm beachy wind. The wonderful sound wrapped around him like a cocoon of gladness. He unwrapped another caramel and popped it into his mouth. He analyzed the sweet, delicate flavors – corn syrup, butter, a bit of salt, sugar…vanilla. He closed his eyes and felt as if he'd taken a trip back in time, back to the days when Mimi was still alive, in their bakery, whipping up her secret sweet candy. "This is delicious. I'll bet your customers love these."

"Actually, they haven't tasted them yet."

He raised his eyebrows and stopped walking. "Are you kidding?" He gestured toward the tourists sunbathing on the beach. "I'll bet these candies would sell out if you sold them."

"Oh, I will sell them. I just want to make sure the recipe is perfect before…well, before I present them to the public." Her smile slowly faded into a frown. Oh no, looked like she was upset. She was probably thinking about her friend Susan.

"Are you alright?" He resisted the urge to touch her shoulder. He kind of liked being around her. Being around somebody who resembled Mimi made him feel glad and spooky at the same time. He needed to make a conscious effort not to read too much into this feeling of gladness that zinged through him like a lightening bolt. He needed to remember that this beautiful woman was *not* Mimi.

"I'm fine. It's just that…" She slowly strolled again. She removed her flip flops and ambled toward the edge of the water. She bathed her feet and he followed her lead and removed his sandals as well. The cool wet water glided over his feet. He squished his toes into the damp sand. She sighed. "Well, my candy shop. It hasn't been doing so great lately." She then went on to describe the financial problems of her shop and she also told him about the last conversation she'd had with Susan right before she'd had her stroke. "I felt as if she was going to tell me something. I hope she starts talking soon."

He nodded, feeling bad for her. He gave her a sideways glance. "So, is Lyle going to continue to help you in the candy store while your friend is in the hospital?" He didn't bother telling her that he'd been visiting the candy store frequently while she'd been gone. He figured Lyle may have already mentioned that to her.

"Lyle has to run his own handyman business. He had some free time to help me this week, but, next week he's fully booked. When he stops helping out, I'll be even more short-staffed."

"Even more short-staffed?"

She nodded. "We get more customers during the summer. The teenager that we'd hired to work with us for the summer never showed up to work. Now with Susan in the hospital, I'll need to hire two people, I reckon." She took a deep breath as she stared at the vivid blue ocean. Right now, she looked as if the weight of the world rested on her slender shoulders. The urge to help and protect her buoyed inside of him, just like the waves that slowly got bigger and crashed upon the shore. He swallowed. No, he wouldn't offer to help her out. It was already kind of unnerving being around someone who looked like Mimi. Besides, he wasn't here to work. He needed to find Amy Bluestone. He had a mission to accomplish. "Would you be interested?"

When her sweet voice washed over him like a tidal wave, he blinked. It almost appeared as if she were reading his mind, which he knew was totally not possible. He gulped. "Interested?"

"Yes. I don't know how long Susan will be in the hospital. I need help in the candy store and it would be a big relief to have somebody to help who has that kind of experience."

"Well, like I said, I'm not much of a candy maker. I'm a baker."

She shrugged. "I can show you. I think you'd catch on quickly. It just helps that you've had experience in a similar industry."

He took a deep breath. He wasn't sure if this was a good idea. Finding Amy was his first priority. She glanced up at him, her dark eyes were full of anticipation – she wanted him to say yes. He could feel it deep in his bones.

The peal of her phone buzzed from her pocket. "Maybe that's the hospital." She quickly pulled out her phone and accepted the call. "Hello?"

Her eyebrows raised and she smiled, just a bit. "That's wonderful. I'll be there in a few minutes." She pushed her phone back into her pocket. She slipped her sandals onto her dainty feet. "I have to go." She quickly turned and walked quickly toward the shore.

What in the world was going on? He rushed behind her. "Hey, wait up." This spry little lady sure had a lot of energy. He gulped for air as they approached the boardwalk a few minutes later.

She stopped and placed her hand to her forehead. "I don't feel well."

She swayed and Michael rushed toward her as she slumped into his arms.

CHAPTER 6

DARA OPENED HER eyes. She felt the strong pull of muscular arms while the tangy aromatic scent of aftershave surrounded her. She stared into the strong handsome face of Michael Gray. His dark brown eyes shown with concern while he scrutinized her. She ran her tongue over her parched lips. Goodness, she hadn't realized just how thirsty she was. "What happened?"

"You fainted. Are you alright?"

"Yes." She struggled to get up. Michael helped her to stand, still holding her in his strong arms. Warmth and comfort surrounded her from his strong grip. She mentally groaned when he released her. His arms had felt so good and so right around her. Michael stood while concern shined from his dark brown eyes. "I need to get to the hospital. That was Susan's granddaughter. Susan is talking a little. She said a few words. Can you believe that? I have to go see her."

Michael cleared his throat. "You shouldn't be

driving. You just fainted, Dara. You need to be checked out by a doctor."

She stood up straight as she could. "I'll be fine."

He shook his head. "We need to get you checked out in urgent care. After that, let me take you to the hospital to see your friend." Just hearing Michael's strong voice, taking command, made her stop and think. Her husband Jack used to do the same thing. Tell her what to do. It really irked her when Jack had always felt as if he knew what was best.

"I'm an adult, not a child. I can take care of myself."

"My goodness. You sure are stubborn. I'm only trying to help you."

She glanced into his handsome face. She figured she'd only been passed out for a few seconds. She needed to get rid of this chip on her shoulder. Just because a man advised her about what she should do, didn't mean that he was trying to control her and to control her life. She needed to realize that not all men were like Jack. She swallowed. Might as well own up to her bad attitude and apologize. "I'm sorry Michael. Yes, I'd appreciate a ride to the hospital."

Michael nodded, his bald head gleamed underneath the bright sun. "Like I said, you might want to go to urgent care first. Get yourself checked out, then we'll go to the hospital."

Okay, so, his suggestion made sense. "That's fine." She didn't object as he touched the small of her back, leading her down the boardwalk. Her skin warmed from the firm, yet gentle touch of his hand.

"My car's down the street. I'm staying in the cottage near Lyle's for the summer." Hmm. So, he was only here for the summer? He'd mentioned his deceased wife. She'd thought that he was just taking an extended vacation. He'd never answered her question about employment. Well, no big deal. She'd worry about that later. Right now, she needed to get to Susan as soon as possible.

She walked as quickly as she could toward the cottages. Her mouth felt as dry as sandpaper, but she couldn't worry about that right now. He gestured toward the black BMW. "This is my car." He gallantly opened the passenger door and hovered near her, making sure she was okay. His concern was sweet and she again felt bad about initially declining his offer for a ride to the hospital.

She got into the comfortable car. She sniffed. Smelled like he'd just driven this car, brand new, off the lot. She settled into the seat. She buckled her seatbelt and closed her eyes. She still felt a bit under the weather. Hopefully, she'd feel better soon. She supposed it may have been the stress she'd been going through since Susan's stroke.

Michael got into the car. She relished the scent of his cologne while he started the engine. She glanced at his muscled forearms as he pulled away from the curb. She didn't feel like talking right now. She leaned her head back and closed her eyes.

"Dara." She struggled to open her eyes. Man, she was tired. "We're at urgent care." Michael's deep voice sounded like warm sugar. It just wrapped around her tired soul and made her feel better.

He opened her car door for her and offered his hand. She took his hand, glad for the support as she got out of the car. After a one-hour visit to the urgent care center, she discovered that she suffered from exhaustion as well as dehydration. The doc told her to stay home and rest and get hydrated over the next few days. As Michael pulled out of the parking lot of the urgent care center she touched his arm. "Don't forget about taking me to the hospital to see Susan."

He maneuvered the car towards the hospital. He gave her a sideways glance as he pulled into the hospital parking lot. "I know you want to visit your friend, but, the doc said you needed to take it easy. You might want to just do a short visit and then go home to rest."

She shook her head. Yeah, she needed her rest, but, she felt fine now. She'd had her fainting spell only because she'd stayed up late over the last week, worried about Susan. Now that she'd be able to talk to her friend, then she'd be able to rest, knowing that Susan was on the mend.

He stayed close beside her as she walked as quickly as she could into the hospital. "You need to slow down and take your time." Michael advised before he dropped into one of the chairs in the waiting room. "I'll be waiting right here to take you home." He found an abandoned newspaper on one of the tables. He opened the paper and gave her a quick wink.

Good gracious. Was this man actually flirting with her? Well, she didn't have time for flirting right now. She had to go and see her friend. *Lord, help me, Lord help me.* She chanted the words while she rode up the elevator. She swallowed as she traipsed down the hall and entered Susan's room. She then sat beside her friend's bed. "Susan? Your granddaughter called and told me you were trying to talk." Hallelujah, praise Jesus. This was the first good news she'd gotten since her friend had been taken to the hospital a week ago.

For starters, she'd wondered if she'd caused Susan unnecessary worry by requesting they get a candy-making machine. Her friend could crunch numbers like a champion, so, she figured her friend would know if they could afford something. Perhaps she should not have been so pushy with her request. "Susan?" she whispered her friend's name. Susan opened her dark brown eyes and looked directly at her. "Hey, friend," Dara whispered.

"Dara…" the one word uttered from her friend's lips was like music to her ears.

"I'm right here, Susan." She sniffed and squeezed her friend's hand. "Susan, I've been so, so worried about you. I'm so glad your granddaughter called to tell me that you'd been talking."

"Contest…" the single word slipped from Susan's lips. Dara blinked and stared at her friend. The hospital staff had mentioned that Susan's mind may not be as clear as it used to be because of the stroke.

"Contest?" she needed Susan to be clearer. As

she held her friend's hand, she closed her eyes. She swallowed as she recalled the day that Susan had had her stroke. Her friend had been about to tell her something right before she collapsed. What could it have been?

Dara was grateful that nobody was in Susan's room right now since she wanted to spend some time alone with her. Susan opened her eyes. "Dara…it's..okay. Don't…cccry." Dara rubbed Susan's shoulder. It seemed so backwards that her best friend was trying to console her while being a patient in the hospital. *She* should be the one consoling Susan. The tubes and machines surrounding her best friend still unnerved her. She'd just regained some of her speech, but she still could not swallow. A feeding tube had been inserted into her nose so that they could feed her nourishment.

Dara wiped her tears away and sniffed. "Susan, don't tell me not to cry. It's taking me awhile to get used to seeing you like this." She sniffed again. "Lyle's been helping out in the candy store since you've been sick. Also, I'm still trying to perfect my caramel candy recipe. Remember, we wanted to offer a new kind of caramel, try to bring in even more customers?" She grabbed Susan's hand.

Susan's eyelids fluttered. Looked like she was about to go to sleep. Well, that figured. Her friend was probably tired of hearing her talk about the business right now. She probably needed her rest. One thing she knew about herself, she always told things like they were. In her seventy years of life, she'd discovered that sugar-coating the truth

seldom helped when you were in a tenuous situation. It was best to lay all your cards on the table
and simply tell the truth. The good Lord wanted
all His children to be truthful and truthful she
would be, but, she'd try to be as tactful as possible.
"D..Dara?"

"Susan, don't try to talk now. I know you need
to get your rest so that you'll get better."

"N..no. Help…"

"Help?" Dara lifted the nurse call button and
held it up. "Did you want me to call the nurse
for you?"

"N…no…help for cccandy shop."

"Susan, you won't be able to help me in the
candy shop for a while now."

"No." Susan held up her good arm, the arm
which was on the un-paralyzed side of her
body. She pointed toward Dara before dropping
her arm. "You h-hire…h-help." Dara squeezed
her friend's hand. She thought about Michael,
patiently waiting downstairs for her. She'd again
ask about his helping her, even for a little while.
She'd also need to hire another person for their
summer rush of customers. "Contest." The word
squeezed from Susan's lips.

"Susan, I don't understand. What contest?"

"Look…in…my…desk." She then closed her
eyes and her soft snores filled the room.

Dara glanced around the room and spotted a
small chest of drawers beside the bed. She opened
it and rifled through it, finding nothing about a
contest. Good grief, she was still exhausted and
needed some rest. Susan was obviously talking

about her desk at work. Susan's office was in the back of the candy shop. That's where she did their bookkeeping and that's where they held their weekly business meetings. Well, she knew what she needed to do! As soon as Michael dropped her off at the shop she'd go into Susan's office and rifle through her desk until she found the information about the contest.

CHAPTER 7

MICHAEL STOOD UP as Dara rushed from the elevator. It still knocked him straight to his core, whenever he saw her from a distance. As soon as she came closer to him, her resemblance to Mimi melted away like ice during a spring thaw. Yeah, she was definitely a mighty fine-looking woman and he still found it a bit unnerving to be around her.

He'd not even looked, paid attention to any other woman since Mimi had passed. That is, until he'd met Dara. She raised her cute eyebrows. A sheen of sweat shined from her forehead. She swiped the sweat away with the back of her hand. She looked upset. Hopefully she wouldn't faint again. "Are you alright?"

She shook her head. "Susan was trying to tell me something important. Something about a contest."

"A contest?"

"Yes. Could you drive me back home?"

"Sure. What's your address?"

"I live at the candy store. I have a two-room apartment on top of the store. Lyle never told you that I live above the store?"

He shook his head.

She peered directly into his eyes. "You never gave me an answer about working in the candy store. Let me show you around my store while you think about working for me."

My, she certainly was presumptuous. "But, I've seen your candy store."

"I'm not talking about the space where we wait on the customers. I'm talking about showing you my kitchen and the office. I need to get back to the store as soon as possible. Susan gave me instructions to look for something in her desk."

She rushed toward the exit and Michael clapped his hand on her shoulder. She really needed to slow down. Since she'd had a fainting spell, she really needed to take it easy. He certainly didn't want her to faint again. Besides, the urgent care place had said she was dehydrated. Since their urgent care visit, he'd not seen Dara drink anything. He spotted a vending machine in the corner. "Dara, stay put."

"But we really need to get back."

He shook his head. "Just give me a minute." He moseyed over to the machine. He slipped in a couple of dollars and selected a large bottle of water. He returned with the cold beverage. "This is for you."

"I didn't ask you to bring me water." Sounded like she was pretty mad. Well, if she didn't take better care of herself, she might end up in urgent care again.

"You need to calm down and not get so upset. The doc said you were dehydrated. I'm giving you some water. Just accept it and drink it. What's wrong with that?" This woman had some major problems if she got so riled up about his bringing her some water. If her attitude was so negative towards him then maybe he would not be a good fit to work in her shop after all.

She hung her head and stared at the water for a few seconds. Her frown softened and she finally looked up at him. "I'm so sorry. I've just not been myself since Susan's stroke. No sleep. You're just being kind to me. Thank you."

He gave her a quick nod. "You're welcome."

She unscrewed the top and took a long drink. She guzzled half the bottle. Looked like she was really thirsty. That was a good idea he had getting her a bottle of water. Once they'd returned to the comfort of his car, he made the journey to the candy store. He escorted her to the front door and she unlocked it. "Come in."

He followed her into the shop. She turned the lights on. The display cases were empty. He scanned the shop. He'd been in here lots of times, but, never when it was closed. Tables populated the large space and he recalled how this would be a festive shop when it was filled with customers. He sniffed and got a whiff of the faint scent of spun sugar in the air. He again recalled the entic-ing smell of candy that she made.

The echo of a drawer being opened and closed

interrupted his thoughts. He followed the sound to a back office. Dara was pulling open the drawers of a huge desk, mumbling to herself. She pulled out a stack of papers and riffled through them. "Ah, here it is."

She pulled the paper out and she scanned the document with her pretty eyes. She frowned and bit her lower lip. She then turned away from him and ripped the paper in half. She stuffed half of the paper into her pocket before she presented the other half to him. "What do you think of that?"

He didn't even look at the paper she'd handed to him. He wanted to know about why she'd ripped the paper in half and then stuffed it into her pocket. Looked like she was hiding something from him. "Why'd you rip the paper in half?"

"Oh, stop asking questions and read through that. Tell me what you think." Her dark eyes were expectant as she studied him.

He finally looked down at the half sheet of paper. Looked like a print-out of a website. The advertisement was for the Annual Cruise Ship Candy Competition on the Indigo World Cruise Ship. The contest was to take place in four months and the deadline to apply was in one week. The grand prize was forty thousand dollars. Michael whistled softly. "That's a huge grand prize. What are you going to do with the money if you win?"

She stood up straighter. "I've been having financial problems in this shop like I'd mentioned to you earlier. I'm determined to make this business thrive." She went on to explain how she wanted to purchase the candy-making machine for her shop. "The machine is thirty thousand dollars. This prize will be more than enough for us to buy that machine. Once we have it in place, we'll have a bunch of customers and our business will be in the black again."

Michael highly doubted that the candy-making machine would make their business more profitable. "What makes you think this candy-making machine will solve all your problems?"

She narrowed her eyes. "I just know it will. They have them at some of those beach candy stores over in Germany." She plopped down into the leather office chair and turned on the laptop. A few minutes later, she beckoned him over and showed him a video, demonstrating how folks could see the delicious candy being made.

"Michael, you were enticed by the smell of that candy. If you could smell and *see* the candy being made, it would be like you're being beckoned into the place to buy our treats."

"Dara, I don't know…."

"Where's your faith?"

"Huh?" What did faith have to do with candy making?

"I *know* this is what we need for our business. Susan wanted me to go on this cruise and enter the contest to see if we could win the forty thousand dollars. She was probably thinking about it, but didn't want to mention it to me until she was sure." Her voice faltered and she looked away from him. She was hiding something. He again thought about the ripped paper in her pocket.

"Really? I feel like you're not telling me everything."

She shook her head. "I'm telling you what you need to know. Susan probably wanted to try and win the forty thousand dollars to put into our business."

"So, right before her stroke, she was going to tell you about the contest?" Well, he supposed that sounded plausible.

Dara nodded, touching the paper in his hand. "That's right before she had her stroke. I'm in the midst of perfecting my caramel recipe. I can enter it into the contest." She focused on him again. "Can you help me? I know you're not a candy maker – you're a baker. But, your wife baked a similar candy and since you're in a related industry, I'd think that you'd have an amazing palate."

Working here would be a bit uncomfortable. He opened his mouth, about to say no, when she touched his arm. "Don't respond right now. I know we don't know each other very well, but, I have a good feeling about you. I might not show it, but I do. Can you just think about it and let me know in the morning?"

He swallowed as the floral scent of her perfume wafted toward him like a spring garden. He suddenly realized that he could get used to this, standing beside her, making candy all day. But, he still didn't know if it was a good idea. He'd had his own business for years and he'd sold it and was now retired.

Retired.

He wasn't supposed to be working any longer. He was supposed to be relaxing, enjoying his golden years while he fulfilled Mimi's last wishes. But, since he'd shown up on Crystal Beach, just in a few days' time, his life had changed drastically. For the first time since Mimi's death, he'd smelled candy that had reminded him of her. He'd also met an amazing woman who resembled Mimi.

Dara continued to stare at him, awaiting his response. "Yes. I promise I'll think about it."

Whew, the light tang of candy filled the air, and being around Dara…well, he just needed some time alone to process his emotions. He touched her face before he left the shop. When he returned to his car, his phone buzzed. He glanced at the display. A text from Lyle had come through. *Call me as soon as you get this message.*

He called his friend. "Hi, Lyle."

"Michael. What happened?"

"Huh?" What was Lyle talking about?

"You and my grandma were supposed to come over for dinner tonight. You said you'd be waiting for me. It took me awhile to get here and I found both of you gone. There was a candy box on the porch and you two didn't text me or leave me a note or anything."

Michael quickly told Lyle about Dara fainting, their trip to the urgent care center and he mentioned the hospital visit.

"Michael, I'm so glad you were with my grandma tonight when she fainted. What if you'd not been there? What if she hit or head or something and was seriously injured?"

The same thoughts had crossed Michael's mind, too. "I think your grandmother needs to take better care of herself. Now that Susan is speaking, maybe she won't worry as much."

"So, do you know what she and Aunt Susan discussed?"

"I wasn't in the room with her when she visited." He didn't mention his visit to the candy shop or the competition. He wasn't sure if that was information that Dara wanted others to know right now.

"Okay. Glad to hear Aunt Susan is at least speaking now. Hopefully, she'll be able to make a full recovery from her stroke." He paused. "I wanted to let you know something. The landlord for Amy Bluestone's rental just contacted me. He's coming back to the states next month. He wants to meet up with me to go through the house where Amy used to live. He says he wants me to give him an estimate for repairs. He also wants me to clean the place up. I have an idea."

He raised his eyebrows. "Go ahead. I'm listening."

"Well, it appears that Amy and her husband, or whoever was living with her, left the place a mess." That was an understatement. He'd seen the damage to the place when he'd glanced through that dirty window over a week ago. "First thing he wants me to do is go into the house and get rid of all the trash." He paused and took a deep breath. "I figured you could help me clean up if you want. There may have been something left behind, something that would give a clue as to where Amy may have relocated."

Well, he certainly didn't have anything to lose. "Next month?" He thought about it for a few seconds. "That sounds good." He highly doubted they'd find anything, but, he figured he needed to do all that he could to find Amy Bluestone.

CHAPTER 8

*D*ARA WRAPPED EACH *of the caramels with wax paper. She smiled. It felt like a bucket of liquid sunshine had been poured right into his soul while he watched her work. He'd rushed to help her, but, she'd frowned and had slapped his hand away as if he were a bothersome wayward child.*

Hurt, he'd left her alone and when he'd returned, Dara was gone and Mimi now made the candy. She'd smiled at him and had laughingly said she didn't need his help while making her secret candy recipe. He'd been about to argue with her…why couldn't he help her with the candy, just this once?

An infant's cry exploded from an adjoining room. They didn't have a baby. Did they? He rushed into the pink room. The baby girl tried to get out of her crib, crying at the top of her lungs. "Amy, stop crying."

"Amy stop crying." Michael jerked awake. His throat felt funny, like he'd been yelling. He recalled Mimi telling him a time or two that he talked in his sleep whenever he was troubled about something.

Troubled. Yep, he was troubled alright. He eased out of bed. His mouth suddenly felt thirsty for alcohol. Booze usually took the edge off of his troubled feelings. He sighed. He didn't need to be drinking. If he started drinking then he'd not be able to stop. He'd wake up a hopeless mess with a massive hangover. No way would he do that. *Lord, please forgive me for even thinking about breaking my sobriety.*

Maybe he needed a walk on the beach. He checked the clock. Two thirty in the morning. It had been three days since he'd taken Dara to the urgent care center. He quickly rinsed his mouth out with mouthwash and shoved his sandals onto his feet and went out the back door. The waves tossed onto the sandy shore. He looked up at the ink black sky and peered at the stars and the moon. He closed his eyes. *Lord, what in the world is wrong with me?*

"Michael?" He opened his eyes and spotted Lyle strolling on the beach.

"Lyle, what are you doing walking around on the beach in the middle of the night?"

"I could ask you the same question, my friend. Are you having trouble sleeping?"

"Just the opposite. I was in a deep sleep and... well..."

"Did you have a nightmare?"

Well, he wouldn't exactly call it a nightmare, per se. But the dream was weird enough that he didn't want to go back to sleep. "I just had a strange dream. Got a lot on my mind. How about you?"

Lyle shrugged as they continued to walk. "I stay up late sometimes."

After walking for a half hour, Michael took a deep breath as the sweat rolled down his brow. "Mind if we take a short break? I'm not as young as you are, so I need to rest for a spell."

"No problem."

They made their way to the boardwalk and dropped onto a bench. "So, what's up, Michael?"

He blew air through his lips. "For starters, your grandma. I barely know Dara but she's taken residence in my brain and won't leave."

Lyle's loud laughter carried over the sound of the waves and the wind. "Sounds to me like you like her."

"Yeah, guess you could say that, but, I'm not sure if I'm taken with her because of who she is, or because of who she resembles."

"Huh?" Lyle frowned.

"She reminds me of my dead wife, Mimi. She even looks like her a little bit. I kind of feel like I'm with my wife again when I'm with her. So, I'm uncertain as to if I'm smitten with Dara, or, if I'm smitten with the fact that she reminds me of Mimi."

"Are you going to work with her in the candy shop?"

Michael shrugged. "I don't know. Do you think I should?" He wasn't sure why he was seeking the advice of a man who was less than half his age. Usually Michael prided himself in knowing what to do, figuring things out.

"Well, do you want to?" Lyle gave him a frank, open look and crossed his arms in front of his chest. "If the desire is there then why not do it? You can let her know it's temporary, especially since you're retired and you don't even live here permanently." Lyle paused. "Do you think she likes you?"

Michael shook his head. "No, I don't think so. Far as I can tell, she knows that I used to work in a bakery professionally, owned my own business. She wants my help to make her shop more lucrative. My skills are somewhat unique, and she likes that…heck, she thinks she needs that, especially since Susan is in the hospital."

He didn't answer Lyle's question as to if he *wanted* to work in the shop. He honestly didn't know. And that proved rattling, not knowing his own mind.

"Anything else on your mind?" Lyle prompted.

He nodded. "I still wish I could find Amy Bluestone. I know I need to find her and that we're going to be able to search her house in a few weeks. I just wish there was some way for me to know where she is right now. I want to know if she's okay." He paused and took a deep breath. He stared at the sky for a few minutes. "I sort of feel like I'm failing Mimi. I waited a couple of years before going after Amy because I was hurt that Mimi had kept this from me during our entire marriage."

"And now?"

Michael shrugged. "Now, I'm no longer as hurt and angry as I was when she initially died. I just wish there was more that I could do to find Amy while we wait for her landlord to return to the states."

"Hmm." Lyle stared up at the dark sky as if in deep thought. "Have you ever thought about doing a simple search for her online?"

Michael frowned. "I figured the private investigator had already done all of that." He'd certainly paid him enough money to search for Amy. Besides, he no longer owned a computer and he hated using his phone to do extensive searches on the internet.

"Do you have a picture of Amy?"

Michael pulled out his phone and showed Lyle a picture of Mimi's daughter. The picture was old, she looked to be about thirty in the photo. Lyle studied the photo. "She's pretty."

Michael nodded. "She sure is. She looks just like Mimi."

Lyle gestured toward the shore. "Come on, I have an idea."

Curious, Michael strolled along with Lyle back to Lyle's cottage. A few minutes later, they were sitting in his home office. "What are you doing?" He couldn't resist asking since Lyle didn't seem to be explaining himself.

"I figure Amy might be on social media."

He frowned. "Social *what*?" He honestly had no idea what Lyle was referring to.

"You know, Facebook, Snapchat, Twitter… social media?"

Michael shrugged. He'd never been much of an internet person. He only did what was minimally possible to run his business. Since he'd sold his business, he pretty much had stayed away from the internet, except to pay his bills and to use his GPS. Lyle had turned on his laptop and had opened up Facebook. After plugging in Amy's name, a series of pics appeared. "These are profiles," Lyle patiently explained. He scrolled through the profiles.

Michael's heart thudded. "I think I see her."

"Yeah." Lyle clicked on the profile.

It was Amy! Michael's breath caught as he leaned closer to the computer screen.

CHAPTER 9

L YLE STOOD UP and Michael took the recently-vacated seat. He stared at the com-puter screen. Yep, that was Amy Bluestone alright. He closed his eyes. *Thank you, Jesus.* Did this mean that he'd finally found Mimi's daughter? Had his search ended? If she'd been so easy to find, then, why hadn't the private detective told him about the Facebook Page? He clicked through the pic-tures that were attached to the profile.

Lyle cleared his throat. "There's been no activ-ity on Amy's Facebook page for five years. We could email her through Facebook but, I'm not sure she'd see it. Since we're not friended, the email would probably show in her Facebook Message Request folder. Chances are, she proba-bly wouldn't even bother to access that."

"Friended?" He wasn't sure what Lyle was talking about.

Lyle then patiently explained how folks would friend one another on Facebook. While Lyle spoke, Michael looked through the few pictures on the Facebook page. There were ten of them. In each pic, Amy stood alone. In some of the sel-fies, she was smiling or laughing. The last post tugged his heart. *Please pray for me. I'm having a hard time.* After that, nothing.

He took a deep breath as he stared at the selfie of Amy Bluestone. Lyle then spent the next hour showing him how Facebook worked. Amy Blue-stone only had five friends on Facebook. Seemed like her friends didn't have much activity on their pages, either. Lyle then helped Michael to set up his own profile. He then requested friendship from Amy. "I want to send her an email, but, not sure what to say."

"You can send it later through your phone if you want."

Michael shook his head. "I hate using my phone to go on the internet to look at stuff. I hate that small screen. Mind if I use your laptop?"

"Be my guest. But, just in case you change your mind…" Lyle then took Michael's phone and downloaded the Facebook app. He then accessed Michael's profile. "Don't forget your password. If you forget it, you can always reset it. I friended you myself and I also sent out a friendship request to Amy's friends on Facebook from your profile. One of them may contact you and help you to find Amy."

"Thanks, Lyle." They shook hands before Michael trekked to his house. Later, while he sat in bed, he leaned back against the headboard and put on his reading glasses. Squinting, he studied

Amy's Facebook pics. He then again read the last post on her wall. *Lord, please be with Mimi's daughter. Please help her. Amen.*

Dara opened her eyes. Rested, that's how she felt. She'd taken a sleeping pill to help with her insomnia for the last few nights. Before she'd gone to sleep, she'd thought about Michael Gray and about the candy competition. Actually, she'd been thinking about Michael since he'd taken her to urgent care four days ago. He'd not yet said anything about helping her in her candy shop.

She'd also thought about the competition. She gulped as she sat up on the edge of her bed and opened the top drawer of her nightstand. She pulled out the paper she'd ripped from the competition announcement. Michael had been suspicious. Well, she didn't blame him. He knew she'd been hiding something but, she just didn't have the courage to tell him about her fear.

When Susan had printed off the announcement for the candy-making competition, she'd written something in the margin. Dara forced herself to look at Susan's neat handwriting: *Will Dara be able to present the recipe to the judges? What if she gets frightened and is not able to speak?*

Heck, you'd think at seventy years old, she'd have gotten over her fear of speaking to crowds. But, her fear was just as raw and fresh as when she was a kid. When she was in first grade, she was supposed to do a presentation in front of the class. It was show and tell and the teacher had made it mandatory that each student participate.

She'd peed in her pants, literally, in front of the entire room. She'd been so fearful to go back to school after that. The looks, the snickers, the pain and humiliation washed over her again. All throughout school and college, whenever she had to present to class, it had been a nightmare. Once she'd been struck mute, literally. Her voice simply would not work in front of a crowd. There was just something about being in front of all of those people and being the center of attention that bothered her.

Her pastor at Crystal Beach Community had tried to encourage her to lead a women's Bible study. He'd often overheard her encouraging other women, one on one, and quoting scriptures by heart. The thought of leading a Bible study scared the daylights out of her. No way could she do that. Her pastor had patiently wondered about her profession – after all, she sold candies to crowds of people sometimes. She didn't seem very fearful about doing that.

She'd patiently explained that doing her job was different than speaking in front of a crowd. When the shop was full, she was just giving people candy, ringing up their orders, perhaps responding to a few questions. It's not as if she were in front of the room on display, expected to say something to a big group of people.

Crystal Beach Elementary School had invited

her to speak at Career Day. She'd turned them down. How pathetic was that? She was seventy years old and afraid to speak to a group of children. She figured a lot of children loved candy, so, some of the kids may have enjoyed hearing her speak about making her homemade treats. She may have been able to encourage some youngsters to become great candy makers when they grew up. But, she'd been too fearful to be an encouragement to others.

She shivered. Susan had printed off this information about the candy competition two months ago. They'd been talking about their financial situation for a good long while. Susan had probably thought of this as a great idea, but, didn't want to initially bring it up because she knew how much Dara hated speaking in front of people.

Well, could she go through with this? She didn't have long to figure out if she'd be entering. The application deadline was looming fast and she needed to figure out what she was going to do. Yes, she wanted to enter, but, it wasn't cheap. She'd even toyed with the idea of someone going on her behalf. She could easily teach Lyle or anybody else to make her candy and compete. But, according to the rules, the person who created the candy recipe for the competition had to be the one to make the treats in front of the crowd. After making the treats, she'd have to present the treats to the judges. She'd then need to speak about how she came up with the recipe.

That'd be tough.

There were supposed to be at least 200 folks

in that audience. Could she find the courage to do it? She closed her eyes and recalled how her husband had always belittled her desire to own her own business. He'd handled all the finances and had left her in the dark about a lot of things. Yes, her husband had kept lots of secrets from her and when he'd died, she'd felt so foolish, so scared and so alone.

Although she'd loved Jack and still missed him, there were things about him that she did not miss. She didn't miss his insinuation that she needed to stay in the home, working in the kitchen, being a housewife, because she wasn't cut out to work full time. She swallowed and sat up straighter. For goodness sake, she needed to leave these fears behind.

Before going to bed the previous night she'd again looked up the details about the competition online. The entrance fee was one thousand dollars. She'd also have to get a stateroom on the cruise ship. This was extra money to spend that was not in her budget, at least she didn't think it was. The overwhelming intimidation of reviewing the financial figures for her business haunted her.

As she'd fallen asleep, Michael Gray's handsome brown face had popped into her mind like a warm breeze. He'd owned his own business with his deceased wife, Mimi. He seemed sure and strong and she sensed he'd be a good fit for her business. She slowly put the paper back into her nightstand and got out of bed. After she'd washed up and dressed, she went to her adjoining kitchen. She made a pot of coffee. The gentle drip of the coffee maker and the hickory scent of the steaming brew filled her kitchen.

As she sipped her coffee, she pulled her pink book of devotionals from the kitchen drawer. She read the day's devotional while she sipped her coffee and enjoyed a light breakfast. *Lord, please help me. I feel so overwhelmed by Susan's stroke and running my business alone. I need your help, Lord. I just don't want to fail. Amen.*

An hour later, she went down to her shop. Since Susan seemed to be improving, she wouldn't be spending the day at the hospital, instead she'd be working. Lyle had mentioned that he was swamped with handyman jobs and that he'd be busy for a while. So, for the time being, he would no longer be able to help during the day. She'd already placed a Help Wanted sign in her front window and she still needed to perfect her recipe for the vanilla caramels. She'd initially wanted to perfect the recipe so that she could offer them to her customers. However, now, she had another reason to make sure her recipe was perfect.

If she found the courage she'd need to enter the recipe into the competition.

She checked her watch. Well, maybe she had a few minutes before she worked on her recipe and made the candy for that day. She'd sit outside and relax for a few minutes. She opened the front door.

Movement from the corner of her eye alarmed her and her heart skipped as someone sat up on the bench outside of her shop. Nobody was ever on that bench so early in the morning. When she spotted the young woman, her heart tugged with sorrow. The girl looked like she may have been in high school, maybe a bit older, twenty at the most. Her nut-brown skin was flawless in the early morning light.

She also had a black eye.

Dara forced herself to calm down. "Sorry for staring. I didn't know I had company."

The girl stood up and that's when she noticed the young woman's rounded stomach.

She looked about five months pregnant. "I'm not company. My name's Cassie. I'm staying down at the Crystal Beach Women's Shelter." She pointed toward her shop. "I need a job and I saw your help wanted sign. I need to work."

Okay. This was so unexpected. Number one, this girl was pregnant. She was unclear as to if it would be a good idea for this girl to be on her feet all day serving customers. Number two, she was staying at the shelter and she had a black eye. Would her boyfriend, husband, significant other or whomever come find her at the candy shop and raise a ruckus? The last thing Dara needed was to have some lunatic to come into her candy shop and act a fool.

Thoughts of that day's devotional filled her mind like warm sugar. That day's devotion was about Christian charity and helping others. Yes, the Lord would want her to be concerned about her own welfare, yet, she also needed to help those in need.

"You don't want to hire me. I can tell." The girl

spat the words like hard pebbles.

Lord, forgive me. She was judging this girl, making assumptions about her. She looked into the girl's dark eyes. Her frank direct stare made her pause. The girl wanted work and in spite of the circumstances, she needed to be upfront about why she was hesitant. "Don't get upset. Calm down and come inside. Let's chat about this over a cup of coffee."

"I don't drink coffee. Folks told me it's bad for the baby. I'll take a glass of water with a slice of lemon if you can spare it." Dara nodded at the young woman as she followed her into the shop. Feeling a bit unraveled, Dara stopped and sniffed. Whenever she entered her little shop, the scent of vanilla and sugar made her feel a bit better. The weight of the world's problems seemed to dull, just a little bit, with the scent of candy in the air. After she'd gotten their drinks, she gestured for the girl to sit down at the table. She placed the water in front of her.

The girl guzzled the glass of water as if she had not had anything to drink for days. Dara refilled her glass and then brought out an entire pitcher of water. It was best for Cassie to stay hydrated, especially since she was having a baby. "Have you had breakfast yet?"

"No, ma'am. When I left to come here to see about the job, the shelter hadn't served up breakfast yet."

Dara quickly toasted four slices of bread and served it to Cassie with butter and jelly. She also served her some fresh fruit. The girl dove into the food. "Thank you, ma'am." She managed to speak in between shoving the food into her mouth.

While the girl ate, Dara decided to voice her concerns. "So, Cassie, I have to be honest with you. When I hesitated about your inquiry about working here, it wasn't anything personal since I really don't know you. But, you're staying in the shelter and you have a black eye. Are you in any danger? Is your boyfriend or husband looking to harm you?" She'd call the police or whomever she could to help this poor girl, even if she decided not to hire her.

"No ma'am. He's dead."

Dara frowned. "Who's dead?" She wasn't sure if Cassie was speaking of a husband or a boyfriend.

"My boyfriend. We was living together. We were living someplace we wasn't supposed to be living and...well...he was doing stuff he wasn't supposed to be doing. He was in trouble with the police." She shook her head. "After he was shot I had to leave because I wasn't allowed to live there anymore."

Dara frowned. Something didn't add up. "Are you in trouble with the law?"

"No ma'am. The shelter even called to make sure before they let me move in. You can call the director of the center if you don't believe me."

"How long have you had the black eye?" Seemed like if her boyfriend was dead, and he'd given her the black eye, it would have healed by now? Did her boyfriend recently die?

"I got it two days ago. A drug addict came to the shelter. I happened to open the door and she punched me. The shelter director called the police and that person is in jail. My boyfriend didn't give me this black eye."

Well, that explained the black eye. "Have you been taking care of the black eye? Is there any cream or ointment that you need to put on it?" She just seemed so young and she wanted to be sure she took care of herself.

"Yes, ma'am. I have some cream to put on it. I got it from the drugstore."

She nodded. "So, Crystal Beach is your home?"

"No ma'am. I was living in Atlanta. I came here because I like it. I've been here before a long time ago. People are nice and friendly here. This is where I want to live. I used to know somebody who lived here awhile back." Her youthful voice wavered and got emotional as she spoke of Crystal Beach.

Something about this girl tugged at her heart. Perhaps it was because she reminded her of one of her granddaughters. "How old are you, Cassie?"

"I'm twenty." The girl rubbed her stomach as she spoke. "I need to come up with a way to take care of me and my baby."

Dara nodded. It went against her better judgement, but, she knew, deep in her heart, she needed to give Cassie a chance. "Well, Cassie, you're---"

The bell above the door tinkled and she glanced up and spotted Michael Gray strolling into her shop. She'd been so focused on Cassie and her situation that she'd forgotten to lock the door. The candy shop wouldn't be open for another hour.

"Dara, I decided to take you up on your offer. I'd be happy to work for you in your shop and help prepare for the candy competition."

Speechless. She just didn't know what to say. She resisted the urge to hug Michael and kiss his cheek. It was such a joy, indeed, to see him in her shop so early in the morning.

"No, you can't work for her. This job's mine." Cassie folded her arms in front of her and glared at Michael.

CHAPTER 10

"DARA WAS GOING to hire me just before you walked in." A young woman looked directly at him with her dark brown eyes as if she were going to challenge him for the job. No way was he getting into an argument with a young woman over a job that he didn't need. He did wonder how long she'd be able to stay on the job, though. Looked like she was pregnant. Well, Dara had mentioned she'd needed some summer help, so, maybe this young lady was her new seasonal employee.

"Don't get riled up," he said to the young woman. "I'm sure everything will be just fine." He then focused on Dara. He'd shocked her. He could tell. The previous night, after he'd viewed Amy Bluestone's Facebook page several times, he'd fallen into a troubled sleep. He'd dreamed about Mimi and Amy, but, the dream that had haunted him the most was about Dara. She'd been out in the middle of Crystal Beach, flapping her skinny brown arms, swimming as fast as she could. The waves kept splashing onto her. She'd needed some help and he'd been on a boat, right nearby. She'd looked right at him as she tried to tread water. Her eyes had silently pleaded with him for help, but, her mouth had refused to open.

He'd jerked awake, again recalling how Dara had bristled at his purchasing her a bottle of water when they were at the hospital. She'd not wanted his concern and that had rankled him. After thinking about it for a while, he'd finally come to the conclusion that he'd resisted work-ing for Dara because it was the first time he'd been so attracted to a woman since Mimi had passed. He'd felt he was being unfaithful to his wife's memory. Granted, he knew that there was absolutely nothing wrong for widowers to remarry, it was just that…well…what he'd had with his Mimi had been special. So special that it was difficult to express how he felt to others.

Over their decades-long marriage, they'd been through a lot of bumps but, their love got them through so much. His longing for grandchildren tugged at his heart. He again focused on the young pregnant woman standing beside Dara.

She was a pretty little thing, skinny, and her belly was swollen with child. The girl looked like she belonged in high school and the urge to protect her suddenly swelled within him like a slowly growing wave.

He grinned and offered his hand. "I'm Michael Gray."

The girl barely nodded and accepted his hand.

"I'm Cassie and like I already said, this job is mine." He wondered how such a young pregnant woman had happened to appear in Dara's shop for the job, but, he didn't ask her about that right now.

Dara leaned toward him. She grinned. Well, it was nice to see her smile for once. Her lovely brown face was much too pretty to be frowning so much. "Michael, it's nice to see you. Looks like both of you will be working here. At least while Susan is in the hospital."

"Is there any news about her this morning?" The circles were gone beneath Dara's eyes. She looked well rested. Well, that was a relief. She needed a few days off, away from this candy store. The urge to take her to a tropical beach, away from everything, unexpectedly filtered through his mind. He shook the thought away. Although he found himself attracted to Dara, it was obvious she didn't share his feelings. She just wanted some help in running her shop. He imagined she also wanted a discerning palate to help perfect her recipe for caramels for the candy competition.

Dara's phone buzzed. She removed it from her pocket and scanned the display. "That was a text from Susan's granddaughter. They're moving her out of ICU, but, they said she'd be in the hospital for at least another week. That stroke was pretty bad. She'll need to go into rehab once she's released from the hospital." Dara reached over and touched his hand. Just the brief softness of her skin made his heart race like a swarm of butterflies. "Thanks so much for asking about

Susan."

He nodded at her. "You're welcome."

Dara then focused on Cassie. "Cassie, why don't you come into the back office with me. I need to get you to fill out some paperwork before you can start working here." He studied Dara as she went into the office with Cassie. She left Cassie at the desk to fill out papers before she returned to him.

"Michael, thanks so much for agreeing to work with me. I really appreciate it." Her beautiful voice sounded sincere and pleased.

"You're welcome." He paused for a few seconds. He'd had so much on his mind lately that he didn't want to forget to tell her what he'd thought about that morning. "I wanted to tell you something that I remembered…this morning, about Mimi's caramels." He took a deep breath. "When she'd make her candy, she always used vanilla beans. She said it created a more intense flavor than using the vanilla extract. She used to have them shipped straight from Tahiti. They were expensive."

Dara raised her eyebrows. "That's interesting." She'd always used vanilla extract in her candies, but, she'd never used the vanilla beans. One reason why she'd never considered doing that was because of the cost. Susan was always good about keeping them on track with their expenses.

He nodded, his bald head shined through the morning sunlight streaming through the bay windows. "I think it'll make a big difference." He paused and scratched the back of his head. "So,

I guess this means you're definitely moving forward with the competition?"

She nodded. "Yes. I'm going to fill out my application this afternoon and make my travel arrangements. I'm going to be spending a lot of money on this competition, so, hopefully, it'll be worth it."

He kind of wanted to go along with her for moral support. She seemed like a proud woman, so, he doubted she'd go for his tagging along and paying for his own airfare and stateroom on the ship. She'd probably scoff at his idea, and besides, they still didn't know each other very well.

He glanced back into the office and noticed Cassie was still filling out paperwork. Dara touched his arm. "Let me show you around the kitchen."

She walked in front of him and gestured toward the kitchen in the back. He got a whiff of her flower-scented perfume as they entered the large area. He scanned the work space. Wow, what a pretty kitchen. Large copper pots rested on the huge stove. He ambled over to the shelves and studied what she had on hand. Large glass containers of chocolate, both powdered and solid, dominated the shelf space. He then recognized the high-end brand of peanut butter. He then focused on the nuts, so many kinds..brazil nuts, hazelnuts, macadamias, peanuts…

There were also other candy ingredients resting on the shelves, mostly different types of sugar and corn syrup. He flexed his fingers. It had been awhile since he'd been inside a commercial kitchen. He was now itching to get started.

Dara mumbled to herself as she removed corn syrup from the shelf. She then removed heavy cream from the fridge. Minutes later, she had an assortment of ingredients in front of her. "I'm going to make a batch of caramels." He stood beside her as she removed two huge pots from a cabinet and placed them on top of the stove. She gave him an apron and instructed him to wash his hands. She measured out the ingredients into the pots and told him to remove her candy thermometer from a drawer.

Later, as he stirred the concoction on top of the stove, she continued to guide him. "Don't cook that for too long or it'll ruin the candy." Her authoritative tone, her hand gestures, her soft sweet voice…ahh…he could get used to this. Her voice was as sweet as the candy he was stirring on the stove.

At some point during their candy making session, Cassie came into the kitchen. "Watch the thermometer," she instructed as she went to focus on Cassie. While he continued to stir the thick concoction, Dara quietly instructed Cassie to wash her hands and she also gave her an apron. He smiled as he secretly watched her take charge in her shop by showing others what to do. Once they'd finished cooking the batch of caramels, she poured the thick concoction into a pan. "This has to set all day. I'll cut these tomorrow morning and wrap them in wax paper." She took a deep breath. "Even though the recipe has not been perfected, I'm still going to sell them. Folks say my caramels are the best and I figure I might as well sell what I can."

He nodded. "Sounds like a good idea."

During his first day on the job, the day progressed quickly. He discovered that Cassie was intelligent and she asked a lot of questions. Apparently, she'd worked a register before, so, she caught on quickly. He'd been a bit surprised as to how well the three of them worked so well together so quickly. It was almost as if they'd been working together for weeks – it just didn't seem like it was the first day on the job. Perhaps he felt that way because being in a commercial kitchen, making sweets, was somewhat familiar to him since he used to own a bakery.

At the end of the day, Dara told Cassie to go back to the shelter and he assisted her with cleanup. As he hung up his apron, Dara speared him with a look. "So, Michael, what'd you think about your first day on the job?"

He grinned. "I liked it. Actually, I liked it a lot." She returned his smile. The urge to kiss her lips suddenly consumed him. He took a deep breath. No way could he kiss her. Instead, he touched her cheek before he turned and left the shop.

This had been a pleasant day of work. Granted she was just working with Michael and Cassie for the first time but from what she could tell both of them were hard workers. Michael was definitely a great addition to her team and Cassie was polite and eager to learn. Winded, she trudged up the steps to her living space. After she'd showered and enjoyed a light dinner she went back downstairs and sat at the computer in the office. She turned the laptop on and a few minutes later she opened up the application for the candy competition.

She took a deep breath. Could she really do this? *Lord, I really need your help right now. Please give me the courage to fill out this application. Please lift my fears away. Amen.* Her fingers shook. She flexed her hands. She could do this if she really tried. She needed that money to purchase a candy-making machine. She figured after she'd purchased the machine she'd pour the rest of the funds into her business somehow.

"Oh, Dara, stop being so nervous." She spoke the words aloud. "Lord help me." She closed her eyes for a few seconds before focusing on the computer screen. She then filled in her name and address. The application was long and detailed and it was an hour later when she finally signed the application electronically and paid the entrance fee with her credit card. She then spent another fifteen minutes booking her stateroom on the Indigo World Cruise Ship.

Once the entire process was completed she checked her email to make sure that she'd received the confirmation for the application as well as the cruise ship reservation. Good, both of the confirmation emails had been received. She then shut down her computer and returned to her bedroom. She slid between the crisp cotton sheets and closed her eyes. She'd done it. It had been difficult but she managed to enter the candy-making competition.

CHAPTER 11

OVER THE NEXT few weeks, Michael eased into the routine of working with Dara and Cassie each day. He'd sampled so many candies that he feared he'd get a cavity. At seventy-one, he prided on the fact that he still had all of his own teeth, and he was determined to keep it that way. They'd made ten kinds of vanilla caramels and all were amazing. They really had a great weekend when the Fourth of July profits rolled in. Flocks of tourists descended onto Crystal Beach during the holiday week. The beach had been packed and they'd seen lots of folks stopping in to purchase candies. During the night of the fireworks, Dara had stayed open late so that she could serve the tourists who wanted to purchase a drink or a sweet snack.

As he thought about the wonderful holiday week, as well as his newfound addiction to delicious homemade candy, thoughts of Dara clouded his mind. He sliced a sharp knife through a fresh

batch of peanut butter fudge. Cassie stood beside
him, assisting him by spreading a piece of wax
paper between the layers of fudge. He gave her a
sideways glance and caught her open stare.

He smiled at her as she placed the last layer of
fudge onto the pile. They were holding a sale on
peanut butter fudge that day – buy one pound
get one pound for free. In addition to learning to
work in the kitchen, he'd also been assisting Dara
with her finances since Susan was ill. He found
that the shop was barely breaking even, which
was okay. It took at least five years for a business
to get off the ground. Dara had mentioned that
Susan had told her that, but, she still wanted to
see more profitability from her business.

Later that day, as he placed a container of
chocolate buttercreams onto the workbench, he
sighed while he studied Dara as she rushed into
the kitchen to get something. She then quickly
returned to the front of the shop. Cassie arranged
each of the buttercreams onto a decorative display tray. He'd often noticed Cassie rubbing her
stomach, her dark eyes etched with worry. As she
continued placing the candies onto the tray, she
eyed him. "Mr. Michael, I see you watching Dara
all the time. Why don't you ask her out?"

Well, he'd been mulling over that. He'd been
doing some research. Over in Chevy, an upscale
town about an hour away, they had a specialty
store. They sold several kinds of vanilla beans.
Sure, they could order the beans from online and
use them in the candy, but, he felt if they visited
the store and spoke directly to the owner, they'd

be able to find the best bean possible for Dara's recipe.

He never openly answered Cassie's question while they continued to work together all day. Finally, it was four o'clock. Quitting time. He might as well get this over with. He certainly didn't want Dara to make other plans with somebody else. She was a fine-looking woman, so, he wouldn't be surprised if some of the older single men residing in Crystal Beach had tried to ask her out on a date this weekend. Hopefully, he'd beat them to it.

Cassie had already left to return to the women's shelter. Just he and Dara were here now. He needed to ask her this before he lost his nerve. "Dara."

"Yes?" She removed her apron. He ached to touch the curl of steely gray hair that peeked beneath her hair net.

"There's a specialty store over in Chevy. They have all sorts of vanilla beans."

"Chevy? That's an hour away."

"Yeah, but, you hired me because of my sensitive palate. We choose the right vanilla bean for your candy then that gives you more of a chance of winning the contest. Don't you agree?"

She blinked and looked up at him. "Yes, I guess you're right..."

Hmm. She didn't sound very sure. Come to think of it, whenever he mentioned the competition to her, she seemed hesitant about it. Sure, she'd already signed up and made her reservations, but, he sensed that there was something about competing that bothered her. Oh, well, he'd ask her about that another time. Or, maybe she'd bring it up if she wanted to talk about it. "Well, I wondered if we could go out to dinner on Saturday night. My treat. We could go to this nice Italian restaurant in Chevy. We could have dinner after we visit the shop."

Dara looked at him. Her gorgeous brown eyes hesitant. She bit her lower lip before focusing on him again. "Michael, I appreciate the invite. I really do. But, I don't think it's a good idea."

They finished their evening cleanup in awkward silence. Well, he figured she'd say no, but, he just couldn't help trying. He took a deep breath. He was determined to help her. "Even though you don't want to visit the shop and have dinner, you should still use some vanilla beans in your candy. I'll go ahead and get some so that you can try them in your recipe." After all, she needed to go to the competition with the best recipe as possible.

She stopped cleaning the display cases and glanced over at him. "Thanks Michael. I appreciate that."

He gave her a quick nod. "You're welcome."

Dara entered Susan's hospital room. Her dear friend was still hooked up to machines but, at least her eyes were open and she was communicating. Her vision was affected on one side – she saw better on her left side. Dara breathed a sigh of relief when she saw that her friend was awake. "Susan." She sat in the chair beside the bed. An empty dinner tray rested beside the bed. Looked like Susan didn't eat much. The Salisbury steak and mashed potatoes with gravy had been barely touched. Susan no longer needed to be tube fed, which was good.

"Dara." Her friend's eyes widened. "Glad..to.. see…you."

"Good to see you too. Are you feeling better?"

"Okay. Could…be…better." Susan's eyes focused on her with razor-sharp intensity.

"Why are you looking at me like that, Susan?"

"What…What's…wrong?"

Well, that was a loaded question if she ever heard one. Her heart had been topsy-turvy all week. Michael had asked her out on a date this Saturday and she'd turned him down. She'd hurt his feelings, she could tell. Only problem was, she *did* want to go out with him. Michael was nice, kind, caring and he made her smile. Over the last two weeks she'd gotten used to his working in her shop. She looked forward to seeing him each day. She loved being with him. She also enjoyed all of the suggestions he'd made about her candy. Now, she just needed to figure out what she needed to do.

She licked her lips and took a deep breath. She then spilled everything out to Susan. She told her about her conflicting feelings about Michael, and she also told about how he'd come to ask her out on a date this coming Saturday. "Susan, I like Michael. But, I'm not sure if I'm ready for this. I was married for most of my life and you know how much I craved freedom. Jack was so over-bearing. Sometimes, he acted like I didn't have the brains to make decisions for myself. Now that I'm alone, without having to answer to a husband, I'm not sure if I want to start dating someone. Do you know what I mean?"

Susan opened her mouth, closed it. Her eyes fluttered as if she were battling fatigue. Oh great, she had to go and tell Susan all about Michael. Her poor friend was sick, and now she was also bored from hearing her complain about Michael. Susan slowly focused on Dara again. "Go."

Oh, great. Susan was so tired that she didn't even want any visitors now. Dara checked her watch. She'd been sitting there talking to Susan about Michael for over an hour. Her friend was now plumb tuckered out from all of her talking. Yeah, Susan needed her rest and simply did not have the energy to listen to her talk about Michael anymore.

Dara lifted her purse and swung it over her shoulder. "Okay, I'm going Susan. We can talk later when you're not so tired."

Susan slowly shook her head as she focused on Dara again. "No…you need to…go…on…date with..Michael."

So, her friend was advising her to go out on a date with Michael. For real? She glanced at Susan and her soft snores filled the room. Well, looked like she'd be going out on a date with Michael.

Now, she just needed to find the courage to tell him that she'd changed her mind. Hopefully, he'd not found another date for Saturday night.

CHAPTER 12

MICHAEL PEDALED HIS bike until he'd reached Dara's candy shop. He put his bike aside and locked it onto the nearby railing. He'd rented the bike for the rest of the summer. This was the first time he'd ridden one since Mimi's death. Before her cancer diagnosis, they'd spent many summer days riding together. Since he'd been at the beach, he'd seen lots of couples riding around on bicycles.

As he strolled into the shop, his mind plagued with tons of thoughts. First of all, Dara had not accepted his invite. That was a tough one. He'd sensed a vibe between them, a camaraderie. They got along great working in the kitchen together. For the most part she listened to what he had to say when it came to running her business. He sensed she respected his years of culinary expertise and he appreciated that. But, in spite of their camaraderie, she still seemed hesitant about spending time with him alone.

He'd noticed her brow furrow with worry over the last few days. A few times he'd caught her openly staring at him. He'd given her a few quick winks, letting her know that he'd caught her ogling him. Well, if you could call it ogling. Romance seemed to be something that was different at seventy-one. He found himself kind of anxious to be with Dara, but, now he didn't know what to do about it.

Cassie stood with Dara behind the counter. Dara, in her sweet voice, was explaining how she made their salt water taffy. So far, Cassie had been a good worker. He still wondered what she'd do when her baby was born. Since she continued to stay at the shelter, he had to wonder where she would live.

After they'd had a thriving day selling candies to tourists, he spotted Cassie leaning against the counter, circles under her eyes. "Are you okay?" He came toward her. Hopefully that baby wasn't on the way yet. According to Cassie, she still had a few months to go before the baby would be born.

"I'm just tired." She rubbed her belly. "I wish I could lie down."

Dara placed her arm around the girl. "I have a spare room upstairs. Come and lie down. You can spend the night if you want to."

"But, I can't—"

Dara shook her head. "It's no bother. Come on." Dara's firm tone softened Cassie's reluctance. Soon Dara returned from upstairs where he supposed Cassie was lying down. She removed her apron. "I guess we should clean up."

"How about you go on a bike ride with me? Cassie will be fine upstairs. Just leave her a note, just in case it takes us a while to get back."

She bit her lower lip, looking cute as a button. "I don't have a bike."

"We can rent you one from the boardwalk. We'll only be gone for an hour. I know we need to get back to clean up as you said."

He mentally sighed with relief when she nodded. "Alright."

A few minutes later, they were riding along the biking trail around the boardwalk. The scent of the beach mingled with the tangy aromas of the nearby restaurants. The sun shined from the brilliant blue sky and the clouds were like puffs of promise in the heavens. Yes, it was a good day, indeed, and he wanted to make the most of it. When they returned to the candy shop, they set their bikes against the side of the building.

Michael dropped down on the bench outside the shop, winded. Man, he wasn't as fit as in his early years. Now they had to clean up the shop. Well, he knew his insomnia would not be bothering him this evening. If he had to guess, he'd be sleeping like a baby tonight. Dara dropped down onto the bench beside him. Her walnut brown skin shone in the sunlight. She looked at him, a gleam in her pretty brown eyes. She opened her mouth, closed it. Uh oh, looked like she wanted to say something. "Michael."

He grinned. He needed to put her at ease. She had something to say to him, that much was obvious. He didn't want her to clam up and not confide in him. "Yes?"

"If you're still free, I'd love to visit the specialty shop with you and have dinner on Saturday night." Her brown skin reddened. He wasn't sure if it was the bright sun making her hot, or, if she were blushing. He didn't realize that seventy-year-old women could still blush. He chuckled and just because he couldn't resist, he took her hand. Thank goodness she didn't pull her hand away. He massaged her fingers.

"Yes, I'm still free. I'll pick you up at five thirty. That'll give us plenty of time to get ready after we close the shop."

She grinned and squeezed his hand. He just couldn't stop grinning. He was already looking forward to their Saturday night date.

Dara pulled out yet another dress from her closet. Man, she really needed her best friend right now. Susan was good with coordinating colors and giving advice about fashion. Cassie poked her head into the room. "You okay in here, Ms. Dara? Do you need some help with something?"

She grinned, glad at the interruption. Since Cassie had taken her nap that day when she was too tired to go home, Dara had visited the women's shelter. The director was an acquaintance of hers and she'd freely given Cassie an excellent reference as a roommate. "She's honest and proud. If you do take her in and let her live in your house, she's not going to take advantage of your kindness. She's interested in making her own way. She's just concerned about what to do when the baby comes."

After much thought and prayer, she'd decided to allow Cassie to live with her in the spare upstairs bedroom. Cassie had been hesitant about moving in – she'd wanted to know if Dara was making the offer because she felt sorry for her. Dara had said she'd simply wanted to help and it would be a temporary arrangement. She still wondered about Cassie's family. The girl seemed to be very private and she clammed up when asked too many questions. Dara decided that Cassie would be open to telling her more about her family when she was ready.

She continued smiling at the girl while she rubbed her pregnant belly. "Yes, I could. Cassie, do you realize that it's been decades since I've been out on a first date?"

Cassie grinned. "So, you and Mr. Michael are going out tonight? Took you two long enough to make a date."

Dara shrugged. "Well, both of us are widowed, married for decades. Both of us are older and… well…I can't speak for Michael, but I know how much I'm set in my ways. It's kind of different for me to spend time with a man…well, a man to whom I'm not married."

Cassie came further into the room and pointed to the last dress that Dara had dragged from the closet. "Wear this red one. It'll look pretty against your brown skin."

Dara held the dress up. Her gray hair, dark brown skin, and red dress looked enticing, downright nice. She'd gotten a pedicure earlier, having her toes painted a bright red color – this was the first pedicure she'd gotten in years. She also had some cute white slip-on sandals and a white purse. Since she was wearing flat sandals, she hoped they wouldn't do much walking. She found that she could not walk far in sandals – she needed her walking shoes if they were going to be strolling for a long time.

Well, hopefully they'd do more talking than walking. Cassie exited the room and Dara got dressed. When she came out of the room Cassie smiled. "Ms. Dara, you look so pretty."

"Thanks, Cassie."

The tapping from the front door of the shop caught her attention. She took the stairs as fast as she could down to the front of her store. She glanced through the glass door.

It was Michael.

Her breath caught as she opened the door. His brown skin gleamed beneath the early evening sunlight. He pulled his hand from behind his back and presented her with a dozen yellow roses. The exquisite sweetness of the blossoms surrounded her like a warm blanket. She sniffed. "Thank you, Michael."

He grinned, showing his perfect white teeth. "You're welcome, Dara. You look real fetching in that red dress."

"Thank you." She took the flowers and turned around. Cassie was standing right behind her.

Cassie took the flowers from Dara. She buried her face into the fragrant buds and took a huge sniff. "These smell so good. I thought I'd put these in a vase with some water for you so that you guys can get going."

Dara patted her arm. "That's mighty thoughtful of you, Cassie."

"Hi, Mr. Michael."

He grinned at the young woman. "Hey, Cassie." He then focused on Dara again. "Are you ready to go?"

She nodded. She gathered her purse and keys. He held the door open for her as she exited the shop. She looked back and noticed Cassie grinning at them. The salty breeze whipped around them as he held his hand in the small of her back. They approached his car and he unlocked it with his key fob. He opened the door for her and she slid into his vehicle.

She gulped. Still hard to believe that she was actually out on a date. He started the engine and pulled away from the curb. The beginning of their journey started in silence. She pressed her hands together. She was too old to be nervous – she felt like she was a teenager going out on her first date instead of an old woman with children and grandchildren.

"What's wrong? Cat got your tongue?" His pleasant deep voice filled the car. He grinned at her as he pulled onto the highway.

She returned his smile. "Just seems kind of

weird, us going out like this. We work together every day, but, being outside the shop just makes it feel different."

"Oh, Dara, it's not very different. I'm the same old guy who helps you make those delicious caramels. I've just cleaned myself up and put on some aftershave and put on some fancy clothes."

They pleasantly listened to a jazz station as he drove to Chevy. As he pulled into the lot of the specialty shop, he cleared his throat. "Well, here we are. I already called and told him that we were coming."

"Him?"

"The owner. I wanted an expert on vanilla beans and he's the one. No guarantee that having the right bean will win you the competition, but, it's a good start."

She nodded as he opened her door for her. Her heart skipped as he took her hand and they went into the shop. Herbs and spices filled the numerous shelves. The enticing scents of lavender, jasmine,…she sniffed…and a bunch of other things assailed her nose. It smelled nice, downright pleasant. She could get used to being in a place like this. The polished wooden floor and shelves gleamed as the early evening sun splashed through the windows.

"Good evening." A thirty-something man came from behind the counter. His blue eyes twinkled as he looked at them. "Are you Michael?"

Michael nodded as they shook hands. "Yes, that's me. I want to thank you for agreeing to see us tonight. We really needed an expert."

The young man opened his mouth and laughed. "Well, I don't consider myself an expert, per se, but, I do know a lot about vanilla beans."

Michael gestured toward Dara. "This is Dara. She's the one who needs to know which beans would be best for her vanilla caramel recipe. Dara, this is Tim."

"Nice to meet you, Tim." They shared a hearty handshake before he gestured to the shelves. Clear jars with lids rested along one of the shelves. The elongated dark beans had been shrink wrapped. Each of the vanilla bean containers had the name of a country taped on the outside.

"We've got beans from all over the world. I heard you're making candy?"

"Yes. I want to enter a candy making competition. If I have the best caramel recipe, I'll win forty thousand dollars."

Tim whistled softly. "Wow, that's a lot of loot." For the next hour, he gave a rundown on the best qualities for each country's vanilla bean. They finally decided to try the Madagascar vanilla bean since it had a rich and creamy taste. They also chose the Tahitian vanilla bean because it boasted a smooth floral flavor. They also chose a few others.

Tim placed their purchases into a small bag and rang up the order. Dara cringed at the price. They were spending over one hundred dollars on beans! But, it was worth it since she'd be using it in her candy.

After she'd paid for the beans they exited the shop. Chevy appeared to be a busy town as folks strolled by on the street. Music blared from a nearby bar where a jazz band played. Michael took her hand and they strolled until they'd reached the Italian restaurant he'd mentioned. He released her hand and opened the door for her. "After you."

She couldn't resist smiling as she strolled into the restaurant.

CHAPTER 13

MICHAEL STUDIED DARA across the dinner table. They'd shared a bottle of sparkling cider and had feasted on some of the best spaghetti and meatballs and garlic bread that he'd ever eaten. No wonder this was considered a five-star restaurant. After their server presented them with two slices of cheesecake drizzled with fresh raspberry sauce, Michael leaned toward Dara after their server had left the table.

"After Mimi died I'd hit rock bottom. I need to let you know that I'm an alcoholic. I'd been sober for years." He paused. "I broke my sobriety when Mimi died."

She took his hand. "I'm sorry Michael. I know it must've been rough for you."

He nodded. "Very rough. I just wish I'd had some children and grandchildren to help keep me centered. Yeah, my church family was there for me but I regret that Mimi and I didn't have kids." He sipped from his water glass. "Thank goodness I'm sober again. The urge to drink is there but I'm used to resisting. My life is back on track and I know I need to lean on Jesus for comfort."

She nodded and released his hand. "Amen to that."

He took a deep breath. "So, earlier you told me all about your two daughters and your son." He'd discovered that all of her children and grand-children lived out of the state except for Lyle. Lyle was her son's only child and out of all of her grandchildren she was closest to him. All of her children and grandkids called her regularly and from what he could gather she seemed to have a healthy relationship with them. "You've showed me your kids and grandkids' pictures, told me about their occupations."

He took a bite of cheesecake. The sweet creamy confection blended well with the raspberry sauce. Pure heaven. Delicious. Dara also enjoyed a bite of cheesecake. A crumb from the crust clung to the corner of her mouth. He just couldn't resist. He took his finger and swiped the crumb away. She raised her eyebrows, obviously surprised at the intimate gesture.

He sliced his fork through the cheesecake. But, before he enjoyed another bite, he had to say what was on his mind. "But, I want to hear more about *you,* Dara. Why did you wait until your husband passed before you opened your business?"

Over the next hour, he enjoyed the soft lilt of her voice as she told of her loving yet domineer-ing husband. He inwardly cringed when she told him how her husband often referenced her lack of knowledge concerning money and finances. "I can barely balance my own checkbook, Michael. That's why Susan handles the money and I handle making the candy." She put her fork aside. "I have to be honest with you. I'm scared to death."

He frowned. "What do you mean?"

"I'm talking about the contest. I struggled with entering. I need the money but, I'm not good in front of crowds. It goes back to when I was a child. I've always had a hard time being in front of a big group of people, being the main focus." She cringed and the urge to stand up and protectively take her into his arms and kiss her consumed him. It was terrible that her husband belittled her like that.

He took a deep breath and again focused on his cheesecake. He leaned back in his seat as he enjoyed the last bite of his dessert. He looked at Dara again. The competition stated that the competitors had to make their candy in front of a large audience. They then had to say a few words about how they'd concocted their dessert. Dara was frightened and she needed to see a friendly face while she was in the competition.

He knew she'd already booked her stateroom and paid the contest fee. She really couldn't afford to enter, but, she'd done it anyway since she wanted to win the grand prize. Well, he'd do what he could to help her. They'd already decided that he'd run the shop alongside Cassie while she was away on her weekend cruise. He reached across the table and took her hand. "I'll pray for you, Dara. I'll be praying for you while you're away at the competition." She blinked and looked at their joined hands.

"Thank you, Michael. That means so much to me."

He gave her a quick nod. "I figure it'll be hard for you. Just concentrate and forget about the crowd while you make your candy during the competition."

"Alright."

He squeezed her fingers and relished the softness of her brown skin. "I wanted to tell you something."

She glanced at their joined hands before focusing on him again. "Go on."

He licked his lips and hesitated. It was possible that Lyle may have already told her about his search for Amy Bluestone. Since Dara and Lyle shared a close relationship he was unclear about how much Lyle had revealed about his quest to find Mimi's daughter. "When I told you that Mimi and I weren't able to have children... well..it really affected our marriage. We'd considered adopting but, by the time we looked into doing that, we were too old." He paused as he stared at their joined hands. He then focused on Dara again. She nodded as if she understood that revealing this was painful. "When Mimi died, I discovered she'd had a daughter before we even met." He went on to tell her about his quest for finding Amy Bluestone. "That's why I'm here in Crystal Beach. I'd told Lyle but was unsure if he'd told you about this."

She shook her head. "Lyle's pretty smart. He's not one to tell somebody's business. He probably figured if you'd wanted me to know about Amy, then you'd tell me yourself."

He squeezed her hand. "Knowing about Amy haunted me for a couple of years before I honored Mimi's wishes. I'm now determined to find her." He stared at the table a little while. "I've often wondered if Mimi regretted giving up her only child for adoption and then never being able to conceive again. After I found out about Amy I often wondered if maybe *I* may have been the problem."

"You can't think like that. Don't dwell on the past so much."

He smiled. "That's easier said than done." He stared at their empty plates. "If things go well I might be able to find Amy this summer, Lord willing. Lyle reminded me that next week Amy Bluestone's landlord, the owner for the house where she lived, will be back in town. The landlord will be bringing the keys to the house. I'm going to help Lyle to clean up the place. I'm hoping that I can find something in that house that'll tell me where Amy is. You're welcome to come spend the afternoon with us." He paused for a few seconds. "You don't have to help with the cleaning. You can just sit and visit. I'd love your company. It'll be on Sunday, so your candy shop will be closed."

He sighed with relief when she nodded. "I'd love to come. I'll pack us a lunch to enjoy, too. It'll be nice to spend some time together next weekend." She squeezed his hand. "Thanks for telling me about Mimi and about Amy Bluestone. I kind of sense that it may have been difficult for you to tell about that."

He nodded. "It took me awhile to finally do what Mimi wanted me to do. All that hurt and bitterness festered in me. I had to talk to my pastor a lot about it. It was just hurtful because I wondered if there were other secrets about Mimi that I didn't know about." He shrugged. "I just had to learn to bury my pain and bitterness and move on with my life."

Later, as they stood at the door to the candy shop, he pulled her into his arms. Having her small body in his arms just felt so right. He closed his eyes and kissed her forehead. "Thanks for spending your evening with me." He was already looking forward to seeing her again.

The ship swayed in the wild wind. Dara rushed out of bed and glanced outside at the tossing waves. Her stomach churned as the boat jerked. She held onto her bed. Suddenly she was no longer in her stateroom. She was on deck and millions of people stared at her as if she were some unusual phenomenon. A woman with big lips and craggy hands pointed at her and giggled. Dara stared at the vats of chocolate. Vanilla beans suddenly exploded from the cart beside her. Her ingredients toppled out of their containers while the boat swayed

and the audience laughed while she tried to remember what to do.

How did she make her candies? She crawled on the floor and tried to scoop up the spilled sugar. A shadow loomed above her as someone zeroed in on her for attack. She screamed.

Dara opened her eyes and wiped sweat from her forehead. Her hand shook as she tried to find the glass of water beside her bed. It was still dark and she just couldn't focus on anything.

A knock pounded from the door. "Ms. Dara." Cassie turned on the light and rushed into the room. She rubbed her belly while she focused on Dara. "You okay?"

"Yes, Cassie. I'm fine."

"You don't look fine. Your hands are shaking." The young woman noticed the empty water glass. She took the glass and left the room. She shortly returned with a full glass of ice water. Dara gratefully accepted the cold drink and took several sips. The cold liquid slid down her dry, parched throat. She took a few deep breaths as Cassie plopped onto the bed with her. "How come you keep having nightmares? That's the third time this week that you woke up screaming."

She carefully set her glass onto the coaster beside her bed. "I've just got a lot on my mind, Cassie. Nothing for you to worry about."

Cassie continued to sit on the bed as if she awaited some sort of explanation. "Are you sure?"

"I'm nervous about the candy competition."

Cassie's dark eyes widened. "Is that all? Ms. Dara, you'll be okay. I just know it. Those caramels are so good. You make candy in your kitchen every day. There's no reason for you to be nervous about it."

Cassie really seemed concerned about her and she didn't want to worry her by revealing her childhood fear. After Cassie ambled back to her room, Dara went ahead and got out of bed. It was four in the morning and she doubted she'd fall back to sleep. She decided to go down to the kitchen and bake some rolls for them to enjoy for her lunch date with Michael later that day.

CHAPTER 14

DARA CONTINUED TO think about her nightmare as she placed the fresh home-made hoagie rolls into a plastic bag. She then scooped the tuna fish she'd made earlier into a large Tupperware container. She'd made the tuna fish the night before – it was best to let it refrigerate overnight so that the herbs and spices could marinate into the tuna fish. She then pulled out the cooler and added ice. She then placed the tuna fish, cold sodas and fruit salad into the cooler.

She took her cooler, the hoagie rolls and a huge bag of chips and went to her car. She was scheduled to meet Michael and Lyle at Amy Bluestone's former house that afternoon. She figured they might end up meeting up at Lyle's before heading over to Amy's since he lived next door. She'd brought enough food for Lyle, but, she was hoping that she and Michael could find a quiet corner alone to talk. Lyle was a smart man so she figured he'd give them some privacy while they ate.

While she drove over to the house, she again recalled her nightmare from the previous night. She'd been up since four o'clock and Cassie continued to worry about her. She didn't want Cassie to worry – worry was just plain stressful for an expectant mother. She pushed the thoughts of her nightmare away as she thought about how her week had been going. Ever since she'd gone out on the date with Michael, things had been going well for them. Every afternoon they had lunch together in the office while Cassie manned the shop. She loved to hear Michael's deep, calm voice while he prayed over their meal.

While they shared their daily meal, they got to know each other better. Michael had shared that since he and Mimi had no children, both of them headed the youth ministry at their church. Some of the kids had even thought of them as a second set of parents and they'd enjoyed working with the youth. Michael confessed that after Mimi died, he'd left the youth ministry. It was something that they'd done together for so long that when she'd died…well…it had just been hard to carry on the ministry without her. He'd even been a little sad running the bakery by himself which was why he'd sold it to a young couple whom he'd befriended. She loved hearing about his life and about his days serving in the Navy as a cook.

In addition to their daily lunches, she also enjoyed working with Michael as they continued to perfect her caramel recipe. They'd used the vanilla beans in her vanilla caramel recipe.

The result had been amazing. Michael had also convinced her use the vanilla beans in her chocolate caramels, too. They'd also used imported chocolate in her chocolate caramels, two different kinds of chocolate. Once both of the recipes had been perfected, they'd made a batch of both flavors. Michael had cut the candies and they'd braided them together. The braided chocolate and vanilla candies had been a hit. The two flavors combined were so intoxicating. They'd already had some increase in their revenue from their braided chocolate/vanilla candies. After much discussion as well as prayer, she'd decided that she'd enter the combined chocolate/vanilla recipe in the competition. Since sea salt was sprinkled on top of the candies, and her shop was located near the beach, she'd decided to call her new confection Beach Braids.

She'd brought along a batch of Beach Braids so that Lyle could sample them. Her grandson had been busy lately, so he'd not visited the shop in a couple of weeks. She was anxious for him to try her new candies. As soon as she pulled into his driveway he came out of the house and met her at the car. He opened the door for her and kissed her cheek. "Hey, Grandma. I missed you at church this morning."

She'd been so tired this morning that she'd not gone to church. "I watched the live stream online." It was so convenient for her to watch the service over the internet whenever she was too tired to attend service. Her grandson was scrutinizing her. Goodness, she probably didn't put on enough makeup to hide the bags underneath her eyes. She found it got harder to hide her fatigue as she got older. She didn't want him to ask about her fatigue right now. Instead she quickly opened the back door of her car and pulled out the box of candies.

"I thought we'd enjoy dessert before lunch." She opened the box and proudly presented it to her grandson. "Try my Beach Braids. Michael helped me to perfect the recipe."

Lyle selected a caramel and unwrapped it. He raised his eyebrows when he saw the braided pattern for the candy. He popped it into his mouth and his dark brown eyes widened with delight. "Hey, these are good. This is the best-tasting candy I've ever eaten, seriously."

She grinned. Just hearing her grandson's praise warmed her soul. "I'm entering them into the competition." That is, if she had the courage to go onstage and make the treats and present them to the judges.

"Well, you've got a winner here." Her heart warmed with joy when he returned her smile.

She spotted Michael strolling up the street. He was right on time. They'd agreed to start cleaning the place before they sat down to eat. Lyle disappeared into his house as Michael strolled toward her. "Hi, Dara."

"Good afternoon, Michael."

He pulled her into his arms and kissed her cheek. He then studied her. "You look tired. Are you okay?"

No, she wasn't okay. The urge to tell him about her nightmare the previous night weighed upon her. Well, she might as well be honest with him. She told him about her nightmare. "That's why I didn't go to church this morning. I was simply too tired. That's why I watched the live stream."

Her heart skittered when he touched her face. The warm, loving touch of his gentle fingers soothed her battered soul. "Honey, you need to stop worrying about this. Everything will be okay. Even if you don't win the competition, I'm sure everything will work out. Just leave it in God's hands." God's hands. Yes, she really needed to do that – just leave everything to Jesus. Yes, she really wanted to win this competition so that she could use the prize money for her business. But, if she didn't win, she'd be highly upset...well, at least a little upset. Maybe she was being too hard on herself. She urgently wanted this business to be a raging success. Michael caressed her cheek. "Hey, what's wrong?"

"Just thinking about my business. I still wish it were more successful." Caroline's Candy Shoppe was her pride and joy and she really wanted it to be financially lucrative.

"Why is it so important for it to be a success?" The question caught her off-guard. She figured it was obvious as to why she wanted it to be a success. When folks opened their own business, they were usually trying to make some sort of living.

"What kind of a question is that?" Her voice wavered.

"I was just—"

Lyle strolled out of the house with his toolbox and a ring of keys. A bucket of cleaning supplies had already been placed in front of the house. "You ready to get started, Michael?"

Michael stood up straight and dropped her hand. She already missed his tender touch. She took a deep breath. "I'm more than ready to start, Lyle."

Lyle led the way as Michael and Dara followed behind. She figured they'd remove the lunch fixings from her car once they were ready to eat. They stepped onto the screened-in porch while Lyle unlocked the door. Michael went into the house and Lyle followed him inside. Michael's question as to why she wanted her business to be a success burned in her mind like a boiling pot of candy. Fatigue settled into her bones. She figured Michael and Lyle could clean and do repairs while she rested a bit.

She returned to Lyle's house and took one of his reclining lawn chairs and dragged it next door to Amy's house. She pulled it onto the screened-in porch and laid down. She closed her eyes. "Michael, I think I found something." Lyle's deep voice rushed from the house with the urgency of a speeding bullet. She opened her eyes, surprised that she'd actually fallen asleep. She shook her head and tried to clear the cobwebs of sleep from her brain as she eased out of the chair. She wanted to find out what Lyle had found. Maybe it was something to help Michael find Amy Bluestone.

As fast as her tired legs would go, she entered

the musty house. She sneezed. The dust in the air bothered her. She scanned the mess lying around. Looked like Mimi's daughter was not a very neat person. She found both men in the kitchen. "I heard Lyle yelling. It sounded important."

Michael pointed to a box on the table. "Lyle said he found this in the attic. Looks like some personal stuff in there. There's a notebook with Amy's name on it." He shrugged. "Maybe there's something written in here that'll give a clue as to where she went after she left this house."

She walked toward him and her heart skittered as he put his arm around her waist. Just being close to him put her heart into overdrive. She leaned into him as Lyle removed some other things from the box as Michael opened up the notebook. He flipped the pages. Looked like some simple pencil sketches. When Michael flipped to the last page something floated out of the notebook. Dara stooped over and picked up the cream-colored business card. "Marvin's Mobile Homes." She then recited the address and phone number. She flipped the card over. On the back was a date and time. It looked like an appointment. "May 15th at 3:00."

Michael frowned. "May 15th? That's about a week before Amy left. What do you think this means?"

Lyle emptied the box. "I think it means she had an appointment at that place and that you need to call them. Maybe Amy and her roommate bought a mobile home before they left."

Michael dropped his hand from around her

waist and picked up his phone from the battered kitchen table. He dialed the number. Since he had the volume turned up she vaguely heard the sound of a recorded voice. He frowned as he shut the phone off. "The business is closed for a week for remodeling. The message also said the owners are away for a week's vacation."

"Well, we'll just have to call back in a week. Simple as that." Dara made the suggestion and Michael nodded. But, from the way his mouth was mashed down, she could see that he was upset. Maybe they'd need to drive over there this afternoon, although, she doubted anybody would be there. The address was an hour away. She placed her hand on his shoulder. "Hey, why don't we drive over there this afternoon. I can see you're upset, and I just want you to feel better." She sensed he wanted to at least go and scout out the place. Perhaps there might be somebody around who could help them.

Michael took her hand and focused on Lyle. "You mind if we leave now? I do want to drive over there." She figured Michael asked Lyle if it was okay since he'd agreed to help Michael with cleanup and repairs all day.

Lyle gestured toward the door. "Be my guest. Keep me posted."

As they exited the house, Dara mentally thought about the change in plans. She didn't have her phone with her and she wanted to get a few things before they headed out. "Can you come with me to the candy shop for a few minutes? I just need to get a few things before we leave."

He shrugged. "Sure."

When they returned to the candy shop, she went upstairs as Cassie came out of her room, rubbing her stomach. "You're back from lunch with Mr. Michael already?"

She shook her head. "We had an unexpected change of plans."

After she'd gathered her things she went back downstairs and Cassie followed her.

"Hi, Mr. Michael." Cassie waddled down the stairs.

"Hi, Cassie. How're you doing this morning?"

"Okay." Cassie focused on Dara. "Ms. Dara, where are you and Mr. Michael going? I thought the two of you were going to share lunch."

"Well, we're going on a little field trip. We have some research to do."

The young woman furrowed her brow. "Research? Field trip? Sounds like you're doing a project for school."

Michael clapped his hand on Cassie's shoulder. "Actually, we're looking for somebody. I'm sure at some point you've probably heard me and Dara talking about Amy Bluestone."

The girl's eyes widened as she dropped into a nearby chair. Dara rushed to her side. Hopefully she wasn't about to go into labor. "Cassie, what's wrong?"

"Amy Bluestone is my grandmother. That's why I came to Crystal Beach in the first place. Why are you two looking for her?"

CHAPTER 15

Mᴵᴄʜᴀᴇʟ'ꜱ ᴍᴏᴜᴛʜ ᴅʀᴏᴘᴘᴇᴅ open as he looked into Cassie's soulful brown eyes. He stared hard at her sculpted cheekbones, her full lips, her dark hair. He looked at the young woman the way he'd scrutinize a bug under a microscope. He was searching for some evidence that she was actually Mimi's great-granddaughter.

He took a deep breath as he plopped into the chair beside her. He touched Cassie's hand. Dara pressed a Kleenex into his other hand and he suddenly felt the wetness on his cheeks. He wiped his wet eyes. Cassie looked at both of them before focusing on Michael again. "Why are you crying?" Her voice raised. The girl was scared because she didn't understand what was going on. He'd better hurry up and explain everything to her. Heck, their field trip could wait. Right now, he needed to fully understand Cassie's connection to Amy Bluestone. He also needed her to calm down. No way did he want this young girl going into labor.

He seemed to be having trouble finding his voice. Dara saved the day. She pulled up a chair and joined them at the table. She patted Cassie's shoulder. "Honey, don't get upset. Just give Michael a moment to compose himself so that he can explain everything to you."

"Huh? Can't you explain?" she asked Dara.

"No, Cassie. It's not my story to tell."

Dara grabbed more tissues for Michael. He finished wiping his face as he leaned back in his chair. "Your grandmother, Amy Bluestone, was my deceased wife's daughter." His voice came out sounding gruff. He supposed it was from his tears. "I didn't know my wife had birthed a daughter before I met her. That is, I didn't know until shortly before she died. My wife wanted me to find Amy to make sure she's okay." He paused and gathered his thoughts. Cassie seemed like a nice girl, but, he only wanted to tell her what she needed to know. "I really need to find Amy so that I can give her a letter from Mimi, that's my deceased wife." He didn't mention the money that Mimi had left for Amy. He figured they could talk about that another time, that is, after he found Amy.

He took a deep breath. "So, you don't know where she is, do you?"

Cassie shook her head. "No, sir." She paused and stared at her hands. "My mom's name is Belinda. She had me when she was sixteen. She was a single mother and she didn't get along with my grandma, Amy. She's always dated bad men and we moved around a lot. One summer, when I was about ten, me, Grandma Amy, and my mom all came to Crystal Beach for a week." Her eyes sparkled at she looked up at both Michael and Dara. "It was the best summer of my entire life. My mom and Grandma Amy didn't argue, not one bit. We played on the beach, they read me stories, and…well…they acted like I was the most important person on earth." She took a deep breath. "Well, my mom and Grandma Amy had a big argument when I was in high school and they stopped speaking to each other. When I graduated from high school, Grandma Amy sent me a card and some money. She gave me her address in Crystal Beach." She stopped for a few minutes, as if she had to gather her thoughts. "I left home when I was eighteen to live with my boyfriend." She rubbed her stomach. "The father of my baby. He was a lot older than me and.. well…he was into a lot of bad stuff. After he was killed, I got scared. I didn't want to stay in that terrible environment anymore."

She rubbed her belly for a few seconds. "When I returned home to my mom, I'd discovered that she'd gotten married. Her new husband didn't like my living there. I overheard them arguing about me one night. He hated having me around, so, that's why I showed up here at Crystal Beach. I went to Grandma Amy's house and it was abandoned. Grandma Amy left, and now I don't know where she is."

Michael continued to stare at Cassie. "You don't have a phone number or email address for your grandmother? You have no way of contacting her at all?"

"Yes sir, I did. The phone number I had for her was disconnected. Her email address bounced, too. My mom wasn't too crazy about my contacting Grandma since the two of them weren't speaking."

Michael pulled out the business card and showed it to Cassie. He explained that the private investigator had given him Amy's last known address and that he'd also discovered that Amy was now gone. "We're going to try to find out if someone at this business may have sold Amy, or her husband, a trailer."

Cassie's pretty eyes widened. "Grandma Amy was married?"

Michael shrugged. "Far as I know, she wasn't married. At least the private investigator never told me that. I just know that Lyle told me that the landlord said that two people lived in that cottage, a man and a woman. The woman was obviously Amy. Not sure who the man was." He shrugged. "Could have been a husband. Could have been a boyfriend? Who knows? The PI didn't have record of a marriage license, so, it's hard to say if they got married."

Cassie focused on Michael and asked questions about Mimi. She'd not been aware that Grandma Amy had been adopted. Michael spent the remainder of the day telling Amy all about his life with Mimi. As Dara served them the lunch she'd packed earlier that day, he shared all that he could with Mimi's great-granddaughter. He told of first meeting Mimi at the Civil Rights March in Washington. He showed her the few pictures of Mimi that he had stored on his phone. He also showed her the Facebook page that Lyle had found for Amy Bluestone. Cassie studied the pictures for a good long while.

By the time Michael had finished talking about Mimi and his search for Amy, it had gotten dark outside. Dara's eyes fluttered. The poor woman was tired and Cassie yawned. She'd rubbed her pregnant belly frequently while he'd talked. He'd encouraged her endless questions. The girl had been through a lot and he hoped that meeting him and finding out about his wife, might make her feel a bit better about her life, somehow.

Dara walked him to the door. He kissed her sweet lips and held her in his arms. "We can talk about making the drive to Melvin's Mobile Homes tomorrow morning."

She nodded. "Michael, I know you have a rough time going to sleep sometimes. Pray hard before you go to bed tonight. I know it's been an extremely emotional day for you." He hugged her again before going to his car.

Dara paid close attention to Michael over the following week. She figured he had a lot on his mind since they'd discovered Cassie's relation to Amy. On Monday, the day after they'd discovered that Cassie was Mimi's great-granddaughter, Cassie and Michael had traveled to the mobile home retailer while she'd stayed and manned her shop. Michael mentioned that they'd only found a construction crew on the mobile home site. The crew had simply said that the owners were out of town and that it would be best if they returned next week, after the owners had returned from vacation.

Both Michael and Cassie had been quiet all week. A few times she'd found both of them talking quietly. She assumed Michael was sharing more information about Mimi with Cassie. She knew that it plagued Michael that him and Mimi had never had any children, and she hoped that meeting Cassie would help him. Perhaps he could be a huge part of Cassie's baby's life, that is, if things continued to progress smoothly between them.

Dara still had the familiar nightmare, where she got on stage at the competition and then fainted, or threw up, or simply lost her nerve. She prayed fervently for help. She even visited Susan, who was now in a rehab facility. Her friend's speech was still stilted and somewhat unclear, but, she knew that Susan understood all that she said to her. Susan encouraged Dara to continue to spend time with Michael.

The following Sunday, Dara, Michael and Cassie all attended church together. It had been nice to see Cassie come with them. She'd invited the girl to church a few times but she'd always declined. Dara's church proved to be a nice, supportive network and she hoped that Cassie made some friends at Crystal Beach Community Church.

After church, Michael escorted Dara and Cassie back to the candy shop in his car. Dara glanced over at him. "So, you'll be back to get us in about an hour?" They'd planned to drive back to the mobile home park that afternoon. The owners were supposed to be back by now and they'd had no luck finding anybody by calling on the phone.

He gave her a quick wink. "Sure, I'll be back."

When he returned an hour later, Cassie and Dara got into the car. Cassie made herself comfortable in the back seat. Dara was surprised to see that she'd brought her Bible with her. At church service that morning, one of the ushers had seen that Cassie didn't have a Bible. They'd given her one to keep and Cassie had promised to read it. The young woman opened her Bible. Michael glanced into the backseat. "Cassie, you ever read the Bible much?"

"No, sir. Not at all. It's not something my mom ever talked about doing."

He nodded and gave her a thoughtful look. "Well, you might want to start reading the book of John. You have any questions just ask me or Dara. You can also talk to the pastor at the church if you want."

She nodded as she opened her Bible. As Michael pulled onto the road they started their journey. He didn't play any music that afternoon and she assumed he just wanted silence. Dara glanced into the backseat and saw that Cassie was no longer reading. She'd leaned her head back and dozed.

Soon, her soft snores filled the car.

Michael continued driving along the highway at a good pace. Dara glanced at his handsome profile. It was hard to believe that he'd been working in her shop for about two months now. Around the beginning of June, when Susan first had her stroke, she never would've thought her life would change so drastically. During that time, she'd taken in a pregnant young woman, hired a retired baker, had signed up for a candy-making competition, and had started dating…whoa, that was a strong word. *Dating*. She'd started dating a handsome man who desperately wanted to find his deceased wife's daughter.

She reached over and touched his arm. "Are you okay?" He had that troubled look about him. She realized he still struggled with the fact that he'd waited a few years to continue searching for Amy.

"Just thinking about what I should say when I finally find Amy. I can't just say that I'm her birth mother's husband."

Dara shrugged. It was a good question, but, unfortunately, she didn't have an answer for him. He continued to drive and then she spotted brake lights for several cars in front of them. Michael slowed down and stopped. Traffic had come to a standstill. "I wonder what happened."

"I don't know. Let's try to find out." He turned on the radio to a local station. The announcer told of a big accident on the highway. "Looks like we'll be held up for a good long while."

Cassie yawned from the backseat. Dara glanced

at her and noticed she was just waking up. "What happened?"

Michael told her about the accident on the highway. "Looks like we'll be held up for a good long while."

"Oh…" The girl rubbed her belly and her eyes rounded. Hopefully she wasn't going into labor.

"Cassie? What's wrong?" She couldn't help the urgent tone to her voice.

"I have to go to the bathroom."

She sighed with relief. At least Cassie wasn't having her baby right now. She'd noticed that the girl had to go to the bathroom often. Dara recalled how she'd used to have to use the bathroom a lot when she was pregnant with her kids.

Since Michael was in the right lane, he eased onto the shoulder. "Hold on, Cassie." A few people honked as he drove on the shoulder for a few miles. He then took the next exit and found a fast food restaurant. Cassie made a beeline for the restaurant while he waited in the car with Dara. "I sure can't believe that I'm sitting here spending time with Mimi's great-granddaughter. There's so much that I want to do for Cassie. She's a nice, honest kid and I think with the right guidance she can turn her life around."

Dara turned to look at him. The determined set of his jaw and the sparkle in his eye made her notice just how much he'd come to care for Cassie over the last couple of months. "What kind of guidance do you mean?"

"Well, first off, I need to find Amy. After that, I want to meet Cassie's mom. I want to try and get Cassie's mom and Amy to reconcile. Hopefully, I can get all three generations of women to get along." He leaned back against the head rest and stared out the window. He eyed a family that strolled into the restaurant. "Since I never had kids of my own, I've never cared for a newborn child. Never knew what it was like to be woken up in the middle of the night by a crying infant. I've never changed a diaper, never taken a child to his first baseball game or witnessed a kid cutting his first tooth." He closed his eyes for a few seconds and then he opened them and focused on her. Her breath caught at the intense gleam in his dark eyes. "I want to be a part of Cassie's baby's life. I want to be like a substitute grandfather for that kid. That baby is Mimi's great, great grandchild. I think she'd like it if I was a part of that child's life."

She reached over and squeezed his hand. "I think that sounds wonderful." As Cassie exited the restaurant, she had to wonder if he'd be able to do all that he'd said. Reconciling three generations of women seemed to be a difficult task to pull off.

CHAPTER 16

MICHAEL PULLED INTO THE parking lot of Marvin's Mobile Homes. It appeared the construction crew had finished adding on the rooms to the small office. There was a stark contrast to the white building and then the unpainted offices that had been added to the back. He figured the painting would be done later. He gulped and got out of the car and closed his eyes. *Lord, please help me to find Amy. Please let somebody be here who can assist me. Amen.*

He opened his eyes and spotted Dara, standing right beside him. She smiled and took his hand. Cassie soon appeared beside him. He rubbed her shoulder. "I hope there's somebody here who can help us. If not, we'll just have to call them tomorrow. The message on their voicemail said they'd be back from vacation by now." Well, he supposed they could've waited to call tomorrow when the office was open. But, he just wanted to see if he could find anybody here, right now. He didn't want to wait. Even if there was nobody here, that was okay. At least he'd gotten the chance to spend a lovely Sunday afternoon with Dara and Cassie.

Holding hands, he approached the door with Dara. Cassie followed close behind. Since this was a business, he supposed he could just try and open the door. Office hours were posted on the door and surprisingly the sign stated that they were open twelve to five on Sundays. He put his hand on the doorknob and turned it.

It was unlocked!

Ding dong. The sound of an electronic bell announced their entrance. All of them stepped into a blue-carpeted waiting area. The small open space had two doors which he assumed led to offices. An empty receptionist desk was to their immediate right and black folding chairs lined the perimeter of the room. A large TV dominated one of the walls. The television looked like it was tuned to one of those Hallmark Movies that Mimi used to like.

One of the office doors opened and a middle-aged man smiled at them as he came into the room. Laugh lines fanned from his eyes as he looked at them. "Hi, can I help you?"

Michael swallowed as she dropped Dara's hand and approached the man. He offered his hand. "Hi, I'm Michael Gray." They shook hands. He then took a deep breath and pulled the business card from his wallet. "I'm looking for a woman named Amy Bluestone. She was here last May and it appears she was going to purchase a trailer?" He offered the card to the man.

He flipped the card over and frowned. It appeared as if he were trying to remember. "Are you a detective or the police or something?"

Michael shook his head. He didn't want to mince words. He might as well tell this man everything, just so that he would know how crucial it was for him to find Amy. "My wife died. Found out before she died she had a daughter before she met me. She gave her up for adoption and I promised her, when she died, I'd find her kid to make sure she was okay." He went on to explain how Amy had abruptly left and broke her lease and that they'd discovered that Amy was Cassie's grandmother and that Cassie was also looking for her. "So, you see, it's important that I find her."

The man nodded and scratched his cheek before returning the card back to Michael. "Well, I can tell you this. Amy was here to buy a trailer. She came by herself. Hold on." He moseyed over to the receptionist's desk and pulled out a drawer. "My secretary usually leaves the paperwork for the recent sales in here." He perched a pair of reading glasses on his nose. He mumbled to himself as he flipped through the papers. He finally stopped and pulled out a yellow piece of paper. "Here it is. Amy bought a small trailer. Paid for it with a cashier's check." He recited the address she used for the bill of sale. He wasn't surprised to hear that it was the same address where she used to live in Crystal Beach.

"She didn't say where she'd be living? Why'd she need a trailer? The address she gave you was

her last address and as far as we know, she didn't
tell anybody where she was going." Michael just
couldn't believe that he was still up against the
wall as to how he could find Amy. Maybe he
could contact the private investigator again to
see if he had any ideas as to how to find Mimi's
daughter.

The man shrugged. "I wouldn't know where
she went, but I can tell you this." He stood up and
closed the drawer. "She'd mentioned to me that
she was planning on living off the grid."

Michael frowned. "What?" He had no idea
what this man was talking about.

Cassie touched his arm. "Living off the grid
means she's living someplace without electricity
and stuff."

"Huh?" He'd never heard of such a thing.

The man nodded. "She's right. It's kind of like
living like they did in historical times."

Michael shook his head. He still didn't understand what they were talking about. "I don't
know what you mean." He glanced at Dara and
she shrugged. It appeared she was just as clueless
as he was.

The man took a deep breath. "Usually when
someone lives off the grid, they aren't attached
to a water supply or electricity. They live off the
land. If Amy's living off the grid, she probably
doesn't even have an address, not a physical one,
anyway." The man glanced at all of them. "Hey,
any of you try asking down at the Crystal Beach
Post Office? If Amy's still in the area, she might
have a post office box in Crystal Beach or one

of the surrounding towns. I'd heard that folks off the grid will sometimes rent a PO box, especially since they don't have an official physical address."

Michael frowned. "It sounds illegal."

The man shrugged. "Depends on who you ask. Technically, I guess it's not." He shrugged again. "That's all I can tell you. If I think about anything or remember anything, I can call you if you'd like." Michael wrote his number down on a piece of paper. The man slid the paper into his pocket. They shook hands and he opened the door and held it open for Dara and Cassie.

Once they were settled back in the car he noticed Cassie in the backseat on her phone. Looked like she was texting. Now that he thought about it, he seldom saw Cassie texting or talking to friends on her phone like most young people. "Who're you talking to, Cassie."

"Nobody. I'm just researching living off the grid. Trying to figure out where grandma is."

He took a deep breath and started the car. Dara touched his arm. "Don't worry, Michael. We'll find her." He gave Dara a curt nod before he pulled out of the parking lot.

Dara cut the Beach Braids fast as she could and then set them on a tray. She didn't let the aroma draw her in…she had to be sure she did this quickly.

"Two hours!" Michael clapped as the timer went off.

Dara wiped the sweat from her brow. Whew! What a day. The competition was still looming in the distance. And she still thought about it most every day. Since she knew she'd be nervous around the judges, Michael and Cassie had decided that she could demonstrate how she made her candies in front of them, pretending they were the audience. Michael had come up with this idea shortly after their visit to Melvin's Mobile Homes. He'd even gently suggested recruiting folks in town, or from Crystal Beach Community Church, to come in and be a mock audience for her so that she wouldn't be so nervous during the real competition.

Well, she'd been touched by his idea that was for sure. When he'd told her about doing her demonstration in front of a mock audience, helping her to get used to being in front of a crowd, well, so many things had come into her mind. First off, she'd realized just how much Michael had come to care for her. He was doing all that he possibly could to help her and for that, she was truly grateful. To show her appreciation, she was going to make him a special dinner this coming weekend, making all of his favorite foods.

Michael was really growing on her and her budding feelings for him made her both ecstatic and hesitant at the same time. With longing, she recalled how easily she'd fallen for Jack. She'd been young and naïve at the time and she'd thought he'd be the perfect man for her. Her parents loved him as their own son and they approved of their marriage. Heck, her parents had practically chosen Jack for her themselves since her parents and Jack's parents had been best friends.

Jack had loved her and cared for her. But, he'd put a damper on her independent streak. For some reason, now that she thought about it, Jack seemed as if he may have been intimidated about her having the freedom of working or owning her own business. He'd always said a woman's place was in the home, and she'd wondered if he felt it was his duty to care for her. When their daughters had wanted to attend college, it had been a battle. He said their daughters would marry and their husbands would care for them. She'd had to gently step in and remind him that things were different nowadays. What if a woman never found the right man to marry – she had to learn something in which to take care of herself. Jack was so old-fashioned in his thinking that it had affected their marriage.

Since Jack had died, she found she really enjoyed working in her candy shop. Sure, profits could be better but, she liked making her own money and having her own business. She loved her independence and as of now, did not feel ready to be committed to any man. Yet, her feelings for Michael continued to grow as they worked together each day. She struggled with her budding feelings. Susan continued to advise her to see Michael and she'd enjoyed the time they'd spent together so far.

As she watched Michael and Cassie work

together cleaning up, she took a minute to sit and rest. It had been two weeks since they'd visited Melvin's Mobile Homes. They still had no idea as to Amy's whereabouts. Dara had a friend who worked at the Crystal Beach Post Office. She'd asked and her friend assured her that there was no post office box rented to Amy Bluestone. She still found it odd, downright weird, that she could find nobody in Crystal Beach who had befriended Amy while she'd lived here.

Dara had given the matter serious thought. She'd studied Amy's picture. The woman did not look familiar to her at all. Since Crystal Beach was a small, friendly, beach community, it seemed as if Amy would've had some friends or acquaintances, but, from what she could gather, it appeared the woman had no friends. Both she and Michael had even reached out to Crystal Beach Community Church, wondering if maybe one of the congregation members had known Amy, but, nobody seemed to recognize her.

She sighed. Cassie really wanted her grandmother around when she had her baby, and she really couldn't blame her. Michael stopped cleaning and pulled his phone from his pocket. Looked like he'd received a phone call. He took the call and put the phone to his ear. "Hi, Lyle."

His dark eyes widened and he looked directly at her. "Lyle told me that he's found Amy."

She stood up and rushed over to him, Cassie right behind her.

CHAPTER 17

"**Y**OU'RE SURE YOU found her?" He clutched the phone as he awaited Lyle's next words.

"Yes, I'm pretty sure. Remember when we sent that message on Facebook to Amy?"

"Yes." He quickly glanced at Cassie and Dara while he spoke with Lyle. His heart pounded like a kettledrum. He took several deep breaths. He really needed to calm down. Dara approached him and took his hand. Her sweet floral scent and her kindness soothed his frazzled nerves. He squeezed her hand.

"Well, she sent me an email through Facebook. Here's what it says, *'Who are you and why do you want to friend me?'*"

"Did you respond?"

"No, Michael. I wasn't sure what to say. We're going to have to figure out how we're going to tell her who you are."

Lyle had a point. If he just said he was her birth

mother's husband, would she believe him? Heck, he'd not been thinking clearly. He knew next to nothing about Amy. Well, he knew a few things. The PI had given him a file. Amy had graduated from community college and had held a series of office and blue-collar jobs. She had a child and a grandchild, but, he had no idea as to if she'd be open to meeting him. He then speared a look at Cassie. "Cassie. We need to let your grandmother know that you're trying to find her. She's contacted Lyle through Facebook. I'm sure she'd agree to meetup with you when she discovers you're here. Did you know she had a Facebook account?"

Cassie nodded. "Yeah, but, the last time she checked it was years ago. I'm friends with her on Facebook and I emailed her a few times over the last year but never got an answer." She pulled her phone out of her pocket and her eyes widened. "There's a Facebook message from Grandma." Her dark eyes scanned the display. "Looks like after all this time she finally decided to check her Facebook account today. She left her phone number."

Michael dropped Dara's hand and quickly rushed over to Cassie. He clapped his hand on her shoulder. "Ask your grandma if you can meet her as soon as possible. She needs to know that you're pregnant. I'll come with you and explain who I am in person." He took a deep breath. "I'm not sure if Amy will believe me if I tell her over the phone who I am."

"Mr. Michael, my grandma is sweet. She didn't

always get along with my mama, and…she curses sometimes. Gets mad a lot, but, she's nice. If she'd known I'd be here she would've stayed behind to see me. She wouldn't have left and went off the grid like that." The girl seemed determined to handle this her way, so, Michael figured that it would be best to do as she wished. She knew Amy more than he did.

Seconds later, Cassie had the phone to her ear. "Grandma?" Her voice wavered and she swiped tears from her cheeks. She cried as she told her grandmother about her pregnancy, coming to Crystal Beach, finding the abandoned house and then she stopped speaking. "Uh huh." She seemed to be listening to what Amy had to say. "Okay." She nodded. "Grandma, there's something else I want to tell you. I found out that you're adopted. You never told me that. Well, there's a man here, Michael Gray, he was married to your birth mother." Fresh tears drizzled down her cheeks. "Grandma, he wants to meet you. He has a message for you from your birth mother. He's a nice man, Grandma, he's…well…he's like a father to me." Michael's heart warmed like a bubbly pot of caramel candy. His eyes moistened with tears when he heard Cassie's words.

Dara took his hand and squeezed it. Looked like a good portion of what he wanted to accomplish had been done. He'd found Amy. Now, he just needed to get all three generations of women to reconcile. He had yet to meet Cassie's mom, and that was okay for now. He had to do this a little bit at a time. With the Lord's help, he'd eventually see all three of the women reconciled.

Cassie ended the call. She slowly looked toward him and wiped her wet eyes. "Grandma said she wants to come here to meet us." She slid the phone back into her pocket. "She says she'll be here around two o'clock this afternoon."

Still holding Dara's hand, Michael approached Cassie and took her hand. They made a circle. He swallowed and took a deep breath. Heck, he was nervous, so he really needed to calm down and lay all of his problems at the feet of Jesus Christ. "Let's bow our head in prayer." He bowed his head and closed his eyes. "Jesus, please help me. I'm nervous about meeting Amy. I've been hoping to find her for two and a half months. Now that I'm going to see her this afternoon, I'm... well, I'm scared, Lord. I know how much this meant to Mimi, so, please let your Holy Spirit guide and protect us as we meet with Amy this afternoon. Please open her mind so that she can listen...hear all that I have to tell her about her birth mother. And Lord, please be with both Cassie and Dara. Cassie will be a mother soon, and she needs your strength and guidance to get her through this pregnancy and become a new mother." He paused and squeezed their hands. "Lord, please, also be with Dara. I know she's still nervous about the candy-making competition, so, she really needs your help, too, Lord. Amen."

"Amen." Both Dara and Cassie's soft feminine voices filled the candy shop. Michael's muscles had been as tight as a rubber band. They continued to hold hands and he kept his eyes closed.

A peaceful calmness engulfed his body as he released their hands.

Dara flipped the sign over from OPEN to CLOSED. Except for the time when Susan had had her stroke, this was the first time she'd closed her shop on a business day. She'd already texted Lyle to let him know that Amy was coming later that afternoon. She figured her grandson would want to know about that since Michael was his friend.

She eyed Michael as he paced back and forth in the shop. Cassie stood at the door, anxiously waiting for her grandmother to arrive. It had been two hours since Cassie had spoken to her grandmother. Michael had been pacing, anxiously waiting since then. Sometimes he and Cassie spoke quietly while Dara continued to wait on customers.

An old, battered car pulled up to the shop. "I think that's Grandma." Cassie's voice wavered with emotional excitement as she stood up so quickly that she knocked her chair onto the floor. Needing something to do with her nervous hands, Dara set the chair upright for her while she continued to focus on the glass door.

A mature-looking woman got out of the car. Her brown dread-locked hair was streaked with gray. Small freckles tinted her smooth brown skin and each of her ears had several piercings. She approached the door, her casual dull gray gown flowed in the beachy breeze. Cassie unlocked the door and the woman stepped into the candy shop. "Grandma!" Cassie and the older woman shared a long hug.

"Baby..don't cry. Everything will be okay." The woman comforted her granddaughter. Dara gave them a moment alone while she went into the kitchen and got out the refreshments. She'd pre-pared lunch, but, she doubted any of them would be very hungry. She took her time and placed the sandwiches on a tray. She then pulled out the pitcher of lemonade she'd prepared as well as a bucket of ice. She then ripped open the bag of chips and dumped them into a huge serving bowl.

She took a deep breath before she carried the meal into the shop. She set the items on a table and pulled out a chair for herself. "Lunch is ready if you all are hungry."

Cassie continued to speak quietly to her grand-mother while Michael hovered close by. She was still unclear as to if Cassie had introduced Michael to Amy already. The threesome approached the table. After Michael had blessed the food, Amy speared him with a look.

CHAPTER 18

M ICHAEL MET AMY'S Frank stare with one of his own. When she'd entered the shop she and Cassie had immediately started talking. The girl had been anxious to see her grandmother and she immediately started talking about the problems she'd been having with her mother which had initially prompted her to leave home with her boyfriend. She'd then started talking about her baby and had started rubbing her stomach. She'd placed Amy's hand on her belly so that she could feel the baby move. Cassie was so excited about seeing her grandmother that she'd forgotten about introducing him to Amy.

But, that was okay. His breath had caught when he'd seen the woman.

She looked just like Mimi. Yeah, sure, he'd seen her photos and knew of the resemblance to his deceased wife, but, it was just a bit jarring and refreshing, to see the resemblance up close. No doubt in his mind that this was Mimi's daughter.

She looked just like his wife – except for two differences – Amy's hair was a dusty brown. Mimi's had been dark. Also, Amy had freckles scattered across her face. His Mimi had had a smooth cocoa-brown complexion.

He offered his hand. "I'm Michael Gray." The woman hesitated before shaking his hand.

"Amy Bluestone." They shared a firm handshake before the threesome ambled over to the table. Dara had thoughtfully made them lunch, but, he didn't think he could eat a thing, he was so nervous.

He pulled the chairs out for all three of the ladies before everybody sat down. After he'd blessed the food, nobody ate anything. Well, he figured Amy was probably as nervous as he was. Well, now was the time to discuss why he'd been looking for her for the last two and a half months. "I'm not sure where to start."

Amy glanced at him, her dark eyes apprehensive. A few tears leaked from her eyes. Her hand shook while she swiped the moisture away. "So, you were really married to my birth mother?" She touched his arm. "I can't believe it."

He nodded. He gave her a few minutes to calm down before he spoke. "Well, it's true. You knew you were adopted, right?"

"Yes, my parents, God rest their souls, were always open with me about being adopted."

She focused on Michael. "What was my mother like?"

"Amy, it will take me a long time to tell you all about your birth mother. Since you've been found, I want to be sure we stay in contact with you. I want to get to know you." He paused. "Mimi would want that and so do I. For now, suffice to say that Mimi was the kindest, most beautiful woman that I've ever known. I loved that woman, straight from the bottom of my heart."

"That sounds so touching, to be loved by a man like that." Her voice wavered again. She pressed her shaky hands together until she'd calmed down. "I never really thought about finding my birth mother." She stared at the food on the table for a few seconds. "I used to wonder about my birth mother a lot when I was a kid. But, as I grew up…well, my parents were always good to me, and I figured that I didn't really need to find the woman who gave birth to me. I felt content." She took a deep breath. "I didn't really start thinking about my birth mother a lot until five years ago."

"What happened five years ago?" He recalled that was around the time the activity had stopped on her Facebook page.

"I've always had a difficult relationship with my daughter…that's Cassie's mom. We had a big argument and well…I haven't spoken to her since. I'd wondered if maybe the problem was *me*. Maybe there was something about me, like a personality trait or something that I'd inherited from my birth mom, which made it difficult for me to relate to my daughter." She sighed. "Cassie hasn't had much contact with me since I had the big argument with her mom. I realize I've been hard to reach since I've been living off the grid for the last couple of months."

Other questions popped into his mind. He wondered why she'd broken the lease for the house she'd been renting in Crystal Beach. Why was she living off the grid? Did she have a husband or a boyfriend? Well, he was sure they'd have time to ask those questions later. He wanted to tell her the most important things first, then they could talk about her living situation and other matters.

He stood up and pulled two envelopes out of his pocket. He gave both of them to her. "Mimi wrote you a letter before she died. She wanted me to make sure you received it. The letter is in the white envelope. When she wrote the letter, she didn't know your name. That's why it says 'to my daughter.' I finally learned your name when I re-hired the private investigator to find you a year ago." She stared at the words scrawled across the envelope. She stroked it. She appeared thoughtful and he wondered what she was thinking. He took a deep breath. "Mimi had a bank account for you. The information is in that second envelope."

Her eyes widened. "Bank account?"

"Yes."

"I..." she put both envelopes beside her plate. "I'm going to open the envelopes later. I'll read them when..well, I want to be by myself when I read them." She focused on Cassie. "I promise that I'll share this with you after I read it for myself." Michael could understand that. He figured it was a huge shock to receive a letter and a bank account from your deceased birth mother. "My life hasn't always been the best. I've struggled a lot, made a lot of bad choices. I was shacking up with a man in Crystal Beach. I rented the house and we lived there. He had a lot of wild company, and he could never hold a job. He left me for another woman – we had a joint account and he took all of the money from it." She paused and took a deep breath. "I happened to play the lottery…bought my ticket over in Chevy. I won forty thousand dollars." She took another deep breath. "I'd never had so much money at one time. I'd heard that if I purchased a trailer and lived off the grid, I might be able to support myself with minimal expenses. I bought the trailer and abandoned the cottage I was renting. I figured it was okay since the owner would be keeping my security deposit."

"Grandma, do you have a job?"

She pulled her granddaughter into a hug. "No, baby. Not right now. As you know, I'm an artist. I love to paint, and I've always dreamed about making a living from my art. Right now, I'm living off the land. I don't have a lot of bills to pay, which is a blessing, I guess."

As they enjoyed lunch, Cassie asked her grandmother questions about living off the grid and Amy asked Cassie about her pregnancy. Michael and Dara also joined in the conversation by letting Amy know how hard Cassie worked in the candy store.

Later, before Amy left, she made sure that all

three of them had the number for her disposable phone. She promised she'd visit regularly. She made sure Cassie knew that she wanted to be in contact with her regularly. She hugged Michael and Dara, too.

Michael plopped down at the table once Amy had left. He eyed Dara as she began cleaning up the remnants of their lunch. Cassie had gone upstairs to lie down. She caught his intense stare, so, she abandoned her chore and sat beside him. She took his hand. "Are you okay?"

Was he? Not really. "About as okay as can be expected. I did what Mimi wanted and that's the important thing." But, there was still a lot left to do. He still wanted to get to know Amy better. He also wanted to meet Cassie's mom…he recalled Cassie had said her mom's name was Belinda. He wanted to try and convince Belinda to reconcile with Amy. Amy's life didn't seem very good at all. She had so little, and she was in her fifties. He supposed he shouldn't measure Amy's life based upon her material wealth, but, there was just something odd, and kind of sad, about a woman who lived off the grid, had to watch her money, and who seemed to have nobody to depend on. He had to wonder if Amy's lifestyle may have been why her daughter, Belinda, refused to speak to her.

Well, with a lot of hope and prayer, maybe things could work out between the three women. He certainly hoped so.

CHAPTER 19

OVER THE NEXT month, Dara continued to sell her Beach Braids in her candy store. She also tried to assuage her fear of crowds by continuing to demonstrate her recipe in front of her church. She'd often invited her church friends to the candy store to watch. She'd been able to prepare the candies in front of them. But preparing candies in front of her church friends was different than making candies on a cruise ship in front of the judges.

Amy had been stopping by the candy shop regularly. She'd been glad to see Amy bonding with Cassie and Michael. Amy had even asked for Michael's help. It appeared that Mimi had left Amy a sizeable inheritance and she wanted to know how she could make her life better without wasting the money. She was giving her situation serious thought and Michael had suggested that they look into options together.

Dara loved seeing Michael interacting with

Amy and Cassie. She knew it still bothered him, knowing that Cassie's mom was not reconciled with Amy. Prayerfully, they'd reconcile soon. Hopefully, once the baby was born, things would smooth out between them.

Thoughts of Michael hovered in her mind as she prepared to leave for her cruise. Finally, it was Thursday, the day that she was leaving for the ship. She had to take a flight to Florida before she boarded the Indigo World Cruise Ship near Orlando. *Lord, help me. Lord, help me.* It felt weird to leave her candy store for the entire weekend, but, it couldn't be helped. She was sure that Michael and Cassie would do a great job of holding down the fort until she returned late Sunday night.

Michael. She still struggled with her feelings for him. She loved spending time with him. She regularly visited Susan at the rehab facility and she'd advised her to keep dating Michael. She loved being with him, but, she also loved the newfound independence she'd discovered after Jack's death. Michael had been able to extend his cottage rental for another month. She knew he wanted to stick around until Cassie's baby was born.

But what happened after Cassie had her baby and what if he were able to get Cassie's mom and Amy to reconcile? Would he be staying in Crystal Beach? She highly doubted he'd be content with their simply dating – he'd want something more, wouldn't he? Marriage just wasn't in the cards for her right now and…oh, she was jumping the gun. She needed to stop worrying about nothing.

She needed to focus on going on this cruise. As a matter of fact, she needed to be sure she didn't get nervous around the judges when--

A loud knocking from the front door interrupted her thoughts. She quickly zipped her suitcase shut. Who could that be? Michael wasn't due to work for another hour. She dragged her suitcase downstairs and spotted Michael through the beveled glass. He grinned. He must've decided to come and give her a ride to the airport. He was the sweetest man. She opened the door and he pulled her into his arms. "Hi, beautiful."

"Hi, yourself. Did you come early to give me a ride to the airport?" They hadn't really discussed his giving her a ride. She'd just assumed she'd drive and leave her car in the long-term parking lot.

"No, I'm coming with you."

"Excuse me?" She looked up at him. "What do you mean?"

He nodded towards her. "Just as I said. I'm going on this trip with you."

"What?" Had he lost his mind?

"I knew you'd object so, I didn't tell you until now. I realize how scared you were to go on that cruise and compete by yourself. I figure if you had a friendly face in the audience, it would make things easier for you." He grinned. "We've been practicing your demonstration to a mock audience. Well, if you see me in the crowd, it'll be like you're right here in the candy shop, giving your demonstration to a friend."

She blinked away the tears that suddenly came

to her eyes. This was one of the nicest things anybody had ever done for her. "But, this is an expensive trip for you to take. Besides, who'll help Cassie in the shop?"

"Sugar, I don't mind spending my money for this. I booked my own plane ticket and booked my own room on the ship. We're doing this together, and I'll be behind you one hundred percent. Besides, I got Lyle to fill in for me while we're gone."

"Oh, Michael, I.." *I love you.* The words ran through her mind fast as the wind, but she stopped herself from saying them. She wasn't sure if Michael was ready to hear something like that. Instead she hugged him as tightly as she could. "Oh Michael. Thank you."

Lord, help me. Lord help me. Lord help me. Dara chanted the prayer and kept her eyes closed. When the judge started announcing the contestants she opened her eyes and waved toward the crowd as her name was called. Standing on the deck of the ship, she eyed Michael right away, sitting in the front seat. He gave her a slow smile and a quick wink.

It had been a whirlwind for the last twenty-four hours. They'd flown into Orlando and had boarded the luxurious cruise ship. After having an exquisite supper in the dining room she'd

gone to the huge place on deck where the candy
competition would be held. She thought it was
odd that the judges required the contestants to
make their recipe twice. All of the contestants
had to make their candy the night before so that
it could set overnight. Most candy recipes had to
set for some amount of time. They made it the
night before so that the next day the judges could
sample it for the contest. The judges didn't want
the audience to watch when they'd prepared
their candy the previous night.

They were also required to make their candy
again the following day in front of the audience.
That's when she knew her nerves would kick in.
That morning the large main deck had been set
up for all of the contestants. There were fifty contestants and several small stoves had been set up
for their candy-making demonstration. Dara had
not been surprised to discover that she was probably the oldest contestant, far as she could tell. In
spite of Michael's caring support, she'd still been
a mess the previous evening after she'd made her
candy. Last night she couldn't sleep. She'd tossed
and turned and her stomach had soured with
dread.

The following day she managed to stand on
board the deck of the ship. She wore her favorite
apron and her blue chef's hat. She barely looked
at the other contestants who also stood at attention. They patiently waited for the judge to give
them the signal to start. She focused on the waves
of the bright blue water. The ship glided at a nice
even pace. She closed her eyes and silently prayed,

seeking the Lord's strength and wisdom during the contest. *Lord, please help me to remain calm. Amen.*

"Candy makers, you can start!" The announcer's voice boomed across the deck. Her heart thudded as she focused on mixing the whipping cream, sugar and corn syrup together. She looked up and her heart pounded harder while she focused on the strangers sitting in the audience. Her stomach churned with dread. *Dear God in Heaven, I'm about to throw up.* Her mouth soured. *Lord, please help me.* She abruptly turned away from the audience.

"Ma'am, are you alright? Is it too hot out here for you?" One of the judges stood right beside her. His pudgy stomach bulged against the buttons of his shirt. Good heavens, if the man breathed too hard those buttons would snap right off! She smiled and tried to find humor in the situation.

Sweat rolled down her brow. It was a scorcher that day. "I'm fine, thank you." The judge returned to his seat in the judge's stand. She realized that the other candy makers were already cooking their concoctions on top of the small ovens. She was already behind so she needed to speed things up. She forced herself to look at the front row, first seat. Michael was there. He looked so handsome wearing his blue Hawaiian shirt and khaki linen shorts. He grinned at her and winked.

She managed to smile back at him. She then gulped down her stage fright the way one would gulp down a bad dose of medicine. *Focus on the candy.* She blocked out the crowd, the noise, the conversations around her. Instead she focused on the hot sun beating down on the deck. She enjoyed the heat while she mixed her ingredients together.

About an hour later, she poured the caramel and chocolate liquids into trays so that they could set. She took several deep breaths and closed her eyes. The judges led each contestant to the side as he or she finished. About ten minutes after she was done, the buzzer sounded. Looked like everybody finished their demonstration on time. The judges had warned if you didn't finish in time then they'd deduct points off from the final judging.

Once the contestants had returned to their spots near their ovens Dara removed the candy she'd made the night before from the fridge. She couldn't serve the candy she'd just made since it was still hot and had not yet set properly. She then cleanly sliced a hot knife through the cooled candy. She quickly braided the thin strips of candy and cut them into pieces. She then set her Beach Braids onto a white plate for the judges.

The judge who had approached her earlier went up to the microphone. He rubbed his stomach. "The judges and I are ready to sample some candy." He wiggled his eyebrows as he spoke into the microphone. "Now, all of our contestants will approach the microphone and introduce themselves. They'll also tell us how they came up with their candy recipes."

When it was Dara's turn to take the microphone, she whispered a quick prayer before making her way to the stage. Fatigue washed through her just like the pristine waves of the ocean. Man, she needed a nap. She forced her eyes to stay open as she gazed at the crowd as she stepped onto the podium.

Fear slithered through her like an angry snake. She glimpsed into the crowd again. Seeing Michael's handsome face on the front row soft-ened her fear. She forced herself to look into the crowd for a few seconds, and then she focused on Michael as she spoke. "I started making candy when I was a kid. My grandmother, Caroline, showed me her secret vanilla fudge recipe when I was five years old. I often dreamed about opening my own candy shop but, I didn't find the courage to do it until I was widowed." She took a deep breath. "I developed this candy, Beach Braids, using my secret salted vanilla caramel recipe and my chocolate caramel recipe." She focused on Michael. "A friend of mine liked both of them, so, he suggested I combine them into one candy. I'm so glad he did because I've been selling a lot of these candies in my shop."

Light clapping filled the hot breezy air. A relief, a blessed relief that that was over. She sighed deeply as she took the seat on the podium with the other contestants. She eyed the judges while they sampled her candy. She witnessed a few smiles from the judges as they sampled her treats. She noticed the pudgy judge who'd approached her earlier – his eyes widened and he took a sec-ond helping of her candy.

She kept her hands clasped together as each

contestant approached the microphone to tell the story behind their candy recipe. Finally, once all of the contestants had said their speech, the judges congregated near the front of the deck. They'd had a small taste of each piece of candy. Dara wondered how that would feel, sampling so many candies at once. She swallowed while she locked eyes with Michael.

Finally, the judges re-approached the microphone. "Okay. We'll start with the honorable mentions." The pudgy judge she'd spoken to earlier cleared his throat as he made the announcement. "The first honorable mention is Dara Greene from Caroline's Candy Shoppe. Her Beach Braids caramel recipe is so delicious." He dramatically drew out the word 'so' so that it was one long syllable. Light laughter spilled from the audience.

Honorable mention? Really? She clamped down her disappointment. They had fifty contestants, so, to even get any kind of mention was an accomplishment. She squeezed down her disappointment and her fear as she came forward and accepted the framed certificate as well as her check for one thousand dollars. Well, at least she placed. But instead of feeling positive she felt downright miserable. Yeah, she was seventy years old, so, she'd had a lot of disappointments in her life. She knew the odds of winning were against her – look at all these amazing contestants. But, she really wanted to make her business profitable by winning the grand prize. Well, she couldn't let her disappointment spoil the rest of the cruise.

She swallowed as she plopped back into her seat and stared at the framed certificate. Yes, she'd hang this up in her candy shop and she'd use the $1,000 to purchase something nice for Michael and maybe buy a few things she needed for her shop. It had been mighty kind of him to accompany her on this trip.

Later, while she watched the grand prize winner, a twenty-something pretty woman, being presented the forty thousand dollars for her Lavender Fudge, she gulped down her disappointment. She forced herself to stand up and clap along with the rest of the contestants.

CHAPTER 20

THE SUN-KISSED WIND whipped around them like a cloud of gladness while they slowly pedaled their bicycles on a trail near the Nassau, Bahamas beach. "Michael, this is great." Dara's excited tone made him smile. She'd looked downtrodden at breakfast that morning and he'd been determined to make her feel better. His heartrate sped up as they continued to slowly ride. Winded, he finally felt it was time for a break.

After they'd parked their rented bikes, he took her hand and they made a short trek to the Nassau beach. They slid their sandals off of their feet and he held her hand while they moseyed over to the beautiful shoreline. The waves crashed upon the white sand. He stood at the edge of the water and relished the feeling of it washing over their brown feet. The crystal-clear blue water was like liquid sunshine. If he squinted hard enough he spotted some small fish in the water. "This is beautiful," Dara breathed. "Makes me forget about losing the contest."

"Dara, remember the promise we made this morning." He couldn't keep the warning tone from his voice. Earlier that morning, he'd told Dara that he wanted to spend the day ashore on Nassau. He'd only wanted to talk about happy things that day. He was determined to make her feel better. He figured once her mood had gotten better he could ask her his very important question later. The question he wanted to ask her burned in his mind like a pot of boiling caramel.

After the wonderful day they'd spent ashore on Nassau, they returned to the ship. While he got ready for dinner that night he tried to calm his racing heart. He took several deep breaths as he made his way toward the dining room. He stood at the entrance and pressed his hands together. He scanned the folks who breezed into the dining room. Most of the men sported black and white tuxes and the women wore fancy dresses in various colors. Seeing all of the fancy clothes and the happy couples…made him think about Dara. Tonight was formal attire since it was the last night on the ship. He tugged his cufflinks.

Dara strolled down the hallway. She wore a simple black dress and pearls. "Sorry I'm late. Took me a while to zip up my dress."

"That's okay." He swallowed as he offered his elbow. He imagined their sharing a bedroom together as man and wife. Whenever they attended a fancy party or a formal event he'd zip up her dress for her. The thought zinged through his mind like happy sea wind. He smiled as they approached their table.

He pulled out Dara's chair. "You look lovely tonight, Dara."

Her dark eyes twinkled while she looked at him. "Thanks." That night, the crew had converted the dining room into a romantic space. They'd dimmed the lights and placed candles on all of the tables. It had been a long time since he'd had dinner in such a fancy place. Heck, the last time he'd had dinner in a place like this was when Mimi was still alive. They'd celebrated their anniversary at a fancy restaurant the year before she had died.

He gave her a quick wink as he made himself comfortable in his seat. He reached across the table and took her hand. "Dara, I wanted to talk to you about something."

She raised her cute eyebrows and bit her lower lip. Well, maybe asking her about this wasn't such a good idea right now. He knew she'd been upset about getting honorable mention. But, she needed to move forward and still focus on her business. She obviously wanted to be a successful businesswoman. Well, she didn't get her forty thousand dollars. But, it wasn't the end of the world. "Dara, I wish you could've won."

She sighed and squeezed his hand. "Michael, it was silly of me to think that I'd actually win. This was a tough competition. At least I got honorable mention. That's something, isn't it?" Although she spoke those words, her eyes appeared sad.

He leaned closer to her. "Don't get upset about losing the competition. In your own way, you did win."

She frowned and looked directly into his eyes. "What do you mean?"

"You spoke in front of a crowd without getting sick. You kept your calm and you did a good job. I overheard a few people in the audience say that they really enjoyed hearing how much you enjoyed making your caramels." He took a deep breath. "You did a good job with your demonstration. That was a big accomplishment for you. You know how you had mentioned that the pastor of your church had wanted you to lead a women's Bible study but you were scared to do it?"

She nodded. "Yes?"

"Well, that's something you may want to consider doing. Today, you proved to yourself that you can speak in front of a crowd. Now you can take your talent and use it to help others to learn about Jesus. Wouldn't that be amazing?"

Her pretty dark eyes widened. "Do you really think I could do that?"

"Sugar, I *know* you could."

Their shrimp cocktail had arrived. While they ate their appetizer, Dara appeared thoughtful. She had something on her mind and he hoped she was thinking what he'd just mentioned to her. "But, what about my business?"

"What about it?"

"It's still not as profitable as I'd like."

"You're breaking even. That's a great start."

She shook her head. "But I want to be a success."

He sighed. They'd talk about the shop later. After they were served their entrées he took her hand. "Honey, I wanted to talk to you about something important."

"Really? What's that?"

"Dara, I love you."

She dropped his hand and her pretty brown eyes widened. Whoa, looked like she had not been expecting him to say that. Well, he was an honest man, and that's something that Dara needed to understand about him. "Well, I do." He took a deep breath. He needed to just go ahead and tell her how he felt. He swallowed and sipped from his glass of iced tea. "I wanted to know if we could make it official."

She still looked stunned. Good. He probably should've waited until they got back to Crystal Beach before he told her about his feelings, but, he just couldn't wait. "Official?"

He nodded. "Will you marry me?" He slid the velvet box toward her and took her hand. Heck, he would've gotten down on one knee but, with his old joints, he knew he'd have a hard time getting up. "I want a real relationship with you. I'd be honored to marry you if you'll have me."

"Michael, I...I don't know if that's a good idea."

His breath caught. "Not a good idea? Why not?" They had taken bike rides, taken walks on the beach and he'd been helping her as much as he could. They were already courting, maybe not officially, but, he'd held her hand enough for her to know how he felt.

"Well, I like being single, unattached. I was

married for most of my life." Her eyes appeared wet for a few seconds. Looked like she was about to cry. Well, maybe she wanted to marry him too but just didn't have the courage to tell him how she felt. She was scared. Well, if she could nip her fear for crowds then she could overcome her fear of marrying him.

She blinked and focused on him again. "My husband was so overbearing, not letting me make many decisions for myself. I want to be my own person. I like not having a man in charge."

"But, Dara." He took a deep breath. This was not going as he'd originally planned. "I'm nothing like your late husband. You've noticed how well we work together. I know I'm not imagining how well we get along."

"No, Michael, I—"

"Do me a favor. Don't speak."

"You're giving me orders already. I'll speak if I have something to say." She stood up and threw her napkin down on the table. Oh no, this was not going well.

He needed to make sure everything was clear, out in the open, so that there were no misunderstandings. "I was going to ask you to pray about it. That's all. Don't be fearful." Something else weighed heavy on his heart. He needed to tell her this. "You know how you say you want your business to be more profitable?"

She glared at him. "That's the whole point of *having* a business, Michael." Her sharp tone caught him off-guard. He certainly didn't want to alienate her any more than he had, but, if something needed to be said, he figured he needed to be honest about it.

"I think you're so worried about being successful because of your late husband. He never really gave you much credit for your intelligence and you want to prove to yourself that his hurtful words were wrong." He stood up and kissed her cheek. "But, Honey, you are intelligent. You own a nice business that's breaking even. Just give it some time. People like you and you've got talent, too. Don't let the negative things that Jack said affect your life now." He touched her shoulder. "I figure I'll give you a couple of weeks to think about my proposal. If you don't mind, I'd like for you to hold the ring until you make up your mind. I'm going back to my room now, but, I'll see you tomorrow when we disembark."

CHAPTER 21

SILENCE. SHE JUST didn't know if she should speak or not. Their flight had landed earlier that morning and now Michael whizzed down the coastline toward Crystal Beach. Yes, she'd thought about all he'd mentioned the night before. Yes, he was correct about Jack's hurtful words regarding her intelligence.

She'd been glad to finally open up her candy shop because she had always had a desire to do that and Jack had never let her. But, she had never figured that her drive for success was directly linked to Jack's hurtful comments over the years. Deep down did she really wrongfully believe everything that Jack had said? Was she trying to prove to herself that Jack had been wrong? At seventy years old she should know herself better than that. She eyed Michael as he took the exit to Crystal Beach. Was it possible that Michael knew her better than she knew herself? She shook the thought away.

She opened her window and enjoyed the briny scent of the ocean. The cruise had been lovely but it was sure good to be home. Michael pulled up to the candy shop and parked. Cassie stood at the front door of the shop clutching her stomach. Tears rushed down her cheeks. She got out of the car and rushed toward the door. Michael beat her there. She unlocked the door and rushed to Cassie. "What's wrong?"

"I'm getting ready to have the baby. I was just getting ready to call Lyle to take me to the hospital."

Michael gently led Cassie to his car while Dara lifted Cassie's packed suitcase. On the way to the hospital, she texted Lyle. She then took Cassie's phone and accessed her contacts. She called Amy as well as Cassie's mom, Belinda. She figured they wanted to be at the hospital to see the birth of their grandchild.

Two days later…

Michael cradled the newborn baby girl in his hands. Dara swiped away her tears. He was such a gentle loving man. She sighed. Could she find the courage to accept his proposal? She took a deep breath and tried to calm down as she admired Cassie's beautiful baby. There was just something about babies and motherhood that brought on happy tears.

"Ain't she precious?" Cassie's mom, Belinda, stared at her new granddaughter. While Michael cradled the infant, Belinda stroked the baby's cheek. "What 'cha gonna name her, Cassie?"

Amy placed her arm around Belinda and swiped tears away from her cheeks. "Yes, Cassie, what are you going to name that precious little girl?"

"I was thinking Belinda Damy Michaela. I want my baby to always remember the people who are most important to me – people who helped me during my pregnancy."

Dara raised her eyebrows. "Damy?"

Cassie nodded. "Damy is Amy and Dara combined." She shrugged. "All of you all helped me so much that I didn't want to forget anybody."

Dara wiped away fresh tears as she kissed the baby's forehead. "Thanks, Cassie."

Michael inhaled and quickly turned toward Cassie. "Is Michaela—"

"Yes, Mr. Michael. I named her Michaela after you." She grinned at him.

Michael looked down at the floor before focusing on the baby again. He stroked her cheek. "You're the prettiest baby…" His voice wavered.

Well, it looked like Michael accomplished want he wanted. It had been two days since little Belinda had been born and during that time both Amy and Belinda had started speaking again after years of silence. No, things weren't perfect between them, but at least they'd openly said that they were willing to work on their relationship. Perhaps the birth of little Belinda would heal the rift between three generations of women.

She'd noticed that Belinda didn't bring her husband with her and she'd informed her that they'd separated. She had started divorce proceedings since he'd been unfaithful to her. Well, at least Cassie could return home without worrying about Belinda's husband. She recalled that Cassie had mentioned that Belinda's new husband had not wanted her living in their home.

Her eyes misted with more tears while she observed Michael. She finally managed to smile at Cassie. "What will you call her? Since your mom's name is Belinda, I figure you'd give the baby a nickname or something."

Cassie grinned. "Well, I was thinking about simply calling her Michaela."

That sounded lovely indeed. She continued thinking about the hospital visit until well into the night. Since Cassie had had her baby, things had been strange at the candy store. She missed having the young woman around. Lyle was not able to help out since he was busy with his handyman business. Both she and Michael still ran the shop and they visited Cassie in the evenings. She often caught Michael staring at her while they worked and she again thought about his proposal.

Well, she loved him, so, maybe she needed to just tell him that they should date regularly and see what happened from there. She still thought about his words regarding Jack. The next day after work she drove over to see Susan at the rehab center. She entered her friend's room and spotted Lyle sitting beside Susan's bed. "Hey, Grandma."

Her grandson got out of the chair and pulled her into a hug. "You look a little bit upset right now. Is everything okay with Cassie and her baby?"

She told Lyle about Cassie having her baby and her grandson had said he'd briefly visited the day after Cassie had given birth. "Oh, they're fine." Lyle gestured toward the only chair in the room for her to sit. She plopped into the chair and took Susan's hand.

Susan was sitting up in bed watching a sitcom on TV. "H..Hi."

"Hi, Susan. How's your physical therapy going?"

"G..good."

Lyle leaned against the wall and observed her. "What's eating at you Grandma?"

Susan nodded. "W..what's…the…matter?"

Was her distress so obvious? Well, she supposed she'd been a big mess since Michael's proposal.

"So, what's going to happen to Cassie now? Is she going to move back in with her mom?"

Cassie's mother lived three hours away. With the new baby there was no way that Cassie could work in the candy store, at least not for the time being. "Yes, she's returning home with her mother but she told me that she's determined to find a job. Belinda has a friend who owns a day-care. She told me that the woman needs to hire a second person to help and she's willing to give Cassie a chance. Cassie could still bring her baby and care for her while she cares for other kids in the daycare."

"T..that…sounds…good." Susan nodded.

"When does this new job start?"

She shrugged. "Not for a few months. Cassie still needs to recuperate and take care of her baby before she starts working." She'd noticed Michael and Amy quietly talking while they were at the hospital. Amy wanted to get her life back on track again. She was going to use some of the money she'd inherited from Mimi to try and figure out what to do with her life. Belinda had offered for Amy to come and live with them. Amy had agreed to visit for a few weeks to see how that worked for them. The three women still had to work through their issues. *Lord, please help them.* She figured it might be difficult for them to be living under one roof, so, she could understand why Amy had agreed to only stay for a few weeks.

"Grandma, are you *sure* everything is okay? Seems like both you and Michael are acting so weird."

She narrowed her eyes. "What do you mean?"

Lyle shrugged. "Well, both of you have been moody. Michael visited my house last night. Seemed like something was on his mind, but, he didn't talk much. I'd just assumed he was kind of emotional because Cassie's baby had been born. He'd told me once that he'd always wanted a daughter."

Well, she might as well tell them the truth. No need to hide it. "Well…" she quickly glanced at Lyle and then Susan. "Michael asked me to marry him."

Lyle's eyes widened. "So, you're engaged?" His loud voice bounced off the walls. "Michael didn't say a word about that."

She shook her head. "I didn't accept his proposal."

He frowned. "Why not?"

"Oh, you wouldn't understand. You're too young and you've never been married."

"Grandma, you're always saying how perceptive I am. You say I act older than my age."

She eyed Susan. Her friend nodded. "Tell… him…yes."

"But, Susan, you remember how Jack used to dominate my life. I like being free without being attached to a man."

"Grandma, Michael is nothing like Grandpa. He'll let you be free. He'll help you to fulfill your dreams. He's not going to belittle your dreams the way Grandpa did." Lyle leaned over and pulled her into a hug. "I think you should marry him."

"Do…you…love…him?"

She ended the hug with Lyle and focused on Susan. "Yes. I love him. I haven't found the courage to tell him that, but, I do love him."

"Then, you should let him know how you feel, Grandma."

After she'd said goodbye to both of them and had returned home, she just couldn't sleep. She thought about all of the changes that were about to take place in her shop. Cassie wouldn't be returning. Michael still worked here, but, his quest to find Amy Bluestone had come to an end. There was no reason for him to stay in Crystal Beach, that is, unless she accepted his proposal. Come to think of it, what would happen to Michael if she accepted? Would he be willing to relocate here, to Crystal Beach, or would he expect her to sell her shop and relocate to his hometown in Twinkle, Maryland?

As she got ready for bed and slid underneath her blanket, she thought long and hard about Michael. He'd done nothing but help her. He'd even helped her to overcome her stage fright. Unless there was some unknown reason as to why he'd want her to give up her shop and move to Twinkle, she knew deep within her heart, that it was just understood that Michael would be moving here to Crystal Beach so that she could run her shop.

She tossed and turned all night and she prayed. *Lord, please help me to make the right decision about Michael's proposal. Amen.*

A loud knock echoed from downstairs. She struggled to open her eyes. Bright sunshine spilled into her room. She glanced at the clock. Nine AM. Well, looked like she'd overslept. She yawned as she finally managed to go downstairs. Michael stood at the door. She opened it. "Michael." She hugged him as tight as she could and he returned her embrace. "I love you."

He then cradled her face in his hands. "Does this mean that you'll accept my proposal?"

She grinned. "Yes."

EPILOGUE

Nine months later…

A CROWD OF PEOPLE hovered in front of the large bay window of Caroline's Candy Shoppe. Dara grinned as she eyed the candy making machine that they'd purchased. Michael was a shrewd businessman and through his contacts, they'd been able to snag a used candy making machine from a store that was going out of business. As the smooth caramel poured from the machine one of their workers spread the satiny sweet concoction onto a large pan. Another worker wrapped the caramels that had been sitting overnight into wax paper. The scent of vanilla and sugar filled the air with sweetness and Dara fondly thought that this was one of the happiest times of her life.

She leaned toward her husband and he put his arm around her. He kissed her forehead. "Did I tell you how much I love you today?"

She looked up at him and grinned. "Yes, you told me as soon as you woke up this morning."

After she'd accepted Michael's proposal they'd had a small ceremony a few weeks later at Crystal Beach Community Church. Amy, Belinda, Cassie, Lyle as well as the rest of their families had attended. It had been a blissfully happy day and she'd not regretted her decision to marry Michael, no regrets at all.

Cassie lived with Belinda and worked in the daycare job that her mom had found for her. She was taking online courses. She said she was determined to get her degree and Michael and Dara encouraged her to continue her studies. They often spoke to both Amy, Belinda and Cassie via Facetime. When things were not so busy in the shop, like during the winter months, they would take long weekends to visit their newfound family.

Amy had managed to purchase a small plot of land right beside Belinda's and Cassie's home. She parked her trailer on the small plot of land and she was happy to have her own place. She was close enough to them to help out with the baby when she was needed. Amy was still determined to heal the rift between her and Belinda. All three women got along, for the most part. They still needed some healing but it appeared their relationships were working out. Little Michaela was cute as a button and Dara loved how Michael doted on the child whenever he saw her.

Susan was out of rehab and was able to get around with a walker. Her speech continued to improve and she'd told Dara that she wouldn't be able to return to Caroline's Candy Shoppe. Michael had purchased Susan's share of the business. So, now she and Michael were partners in marriage and in business.

"You know what, Dara?"

"What?"

"I think Mimi would be pleased with me, right now. I did as she wished and I'm glad I found the courage to do that."

She kissed him. "I think Mimi *is* pleased with you. She's probably looking down from heaven right now, smiling that you found Amy, and that you found a new family. We're all blessed."

He nodded. "Yes, we sure are."

RECIPE

VANILLA CARAMELS

1 and 1/2 cups whipping cream
1 cup granulated sugar
1/2 cup brown sugar (you may use either dark or light brown sugar)
1/3 cup light corn syrup
1/2 teaspoon salt
One whole vanilla bean (if you don't have a vanilla bean you may use one teaspoon of pure, good vanilla extract – do not use imitation vanilla extract!)
1 Tablespoon unsalted butter (plus more for buttering the pan)
Himalayan rock salt or coarse sea salt for topping

Directions:

Line an 8-inch square baking pan with aluminum foil, leaving enough overhang on the sides to easily remove the caramel once it has set. Lightly grease the foil with butter.

Place the whipping cream, granulated sugar, brown sugar, and corn syrup in a heavy saucepan. Split the vanilla bean in half. Scrap the seeds for both halves of the vanilla bean into the saucepan. Place the shells of the vanilla beans into the saucepan. Combine the ingredients and cook over medium heat using a wooden spoon. Keep stirring until the sugars dissolve. The mixture will be thick. When it boils attach a candy thermometer to the pan, making sure not to let it touch the bottom.

Cook and stir gently every minute or so until the temperature reaches 245°F. If this takes a long time then you may raise the heat *slightly* every minute or so until you reach 245 degrees. Immediately remove from heat and stir in 1/2 teaspoon of salt, the vanilla extract (you do not need the vanilla extract if you are using the vanilla bean), and butter.

Pour the hot caramel into the prepared baking pan and top with Himalayan rock salt or coarse sea salt. Allow to cool at room temperature, uncovered, overnight.

Once set, remove the caramel from the pan by lifting out the aluminum foil. Peel the foil off and, using a very sharp knife, cut into rectangles or squares. Wrap with candy wrappers, if desired.

Enjoy! Caramels stay fresh for a few weeks!

ABOUT CECELIA DOWDY

CECELIA DOWDY IS an Amazon bestselling author who lives near Washington DC. She enjoys listening to old tunes with her husband and chauffeuring her teenaged son to school sports events. Baking is one of her favorite passions. She loves experimenting with bread recipes using her sourdough starter. Serving homemade desserts to friends brings her joy. Her love of baking shines in her romance novels. When she's not in the kitchen, or spending time with her family, she's cooking up delicious faith-filled plots. Fans say reading her tasty novels makes them hungry. Sign up for her newsletter.

www.ceceliadowdy.com/sign-up-for-my-email-list

CONNECT WITH CECELIA DOWDY

I HOPE YOU ENJOYED Caramel Kisses.

Join my mailing list for updates about new releases along with fun, inspiring messages:
www.ceceliadowdy.com/sign-up-for-my-email-list

Let's discuss the Bible – visit my Sunday Brunch biblical discussions on my blog:
www.ceceliadowdy.com/blog/category/sunday-brunch

Please visit my website for more of my books:
www.ceceliadowdy.com

You can also find me on social media:

www.facebook.com/CeceliaDowdyAuthor

www.twitter.com/cdnovelist

www.bookbub.com/authors/cecelia-dowdy

OTHER TITLES BY CECELIA DOWDY

THE BAKERY ROMANCE SERIES

Loving Luke *(Book 0)*
Raspberry Kisses *(Book 1)*
Shades of Chocolate *(Book 2)*
Sweet Dreams *(Book 3)*
Sugar and Spice *(Book 4)*
Southern Comfort *(Book 5)*
Sweet Delights *(Book 6)*
Cinnamon Kisses *(Book 7)*

THE CANDY BEACH SERIES

Caramel Kisses *(Book 0)*
Chocolate Dreams *(Book 1)*
Milk Chocolate Kisses *(Book 2)*
Bittersweet Dreams *(Book 3)*
Coffee and Kisses *(Book 4)*
Rocky Road Dreams *(Book 5)*